# GIN & MURDER

*A Violet Carlyle Mystery*

BETH BYERS

# SUMMARY

**September 1924.**

When Violet and Victor are called home to account for their actions, only one course of action is possible. They pack a liberal amount of alcohol and call on their friends to rally round.

They've been outed as writers of sensational fiction! Of falling in love with unapproved individuals! They've bought houses while drunk and had the gall to get sucked into murder investigations! And, it was Violet who was credited with helping to find the killers! The explosion is a story for the ages.

What no one expected was murder. A body soaked in gin is a stretch after what these friends have been through. The real shocker is when the earl asks Jack, Violet, Victor, and their friends to solve the murder and save what remains of the family's good name.

# PROLOGUE

Earl's Children Dishonour Heritage

---

MODERN WOMAN, LADY VIOLET CARLYLE, SCANDALIZES BRITAIN WHEN SHE EMBROILS HERSELF IN MURDER PLOT— INSPECTOR JACK WAKEFIELD STEPS IN TO SAVE THE DAY — HER BROTHER IS LEFT IN THE SHADOWS AGAIN

---

LONDON, SEPTEMBER 2—Recently, Lady Violet Carlyle traveled to Oxford to attend a lecture for the esteemed Hamilton Barnes of Scotland Yard. While there, an unconscionable murder occurred of this journalist's own brother. Lady Violet, using her womanly wiles, bright eyes, and infamous turn of mind, maneuvered her way into the investigation.

Would one say that Lady Violet contributed to the conclusion of the case? Perhaps. The question that should be asked, however, is whether she should have been involved at all.

One might know the history of Lady Violet. Born to Lord Henry Carlyle and the late Penelope Allyn-Carlyle, Lady Violet is the twin to

Mr. Victor Carlyle. The two write disreputable novels under the unimaginative pseudonym, V.V. Twinnings. With such a pen-name, the audience will not be surprised to learn that the books are of unaccountable value.

Would that were all we know of Lady Carlyle. One of many possible heirs of the notable Mrs. Agatha Davies, the bulk of that fortune was given to Lady Violet rather than to the most appropriate of heirs, John Davies, who was the only male progeny of the late senior John Davies. One will remember as well that in Violet's family there were many prospective heirs. If only we did not have to add that Mrs. Davies was sent from this life and fortune as yet another murder victim.

It seems that Lady Violet leaves a slew of bodies behind her, starting with her great-aunt and followed by not one but six MORE murder victims. The claim could be made that Lady Violet was never charged in these murders. Yet, one wonders why she was involved at all.

Mr. Victor Carlyle, twin and stooge, is a lesser heir, a lesser author, and a lesser controller of the fortune inherited, whose only claimable talent is crafting a cocktail.

Does the earl know the shenanigans and mischief his lesser progeny are up to? And if so, will he save our country from them? — E. Allen

# CHAPTER ONE

"Violet, darling! Vi! I'm here. Come kiss me and tell me I'm wonderful." Isolde's voice floated up the stairs to Violet's room, becoming louder with each step. "I have missed you. Oh! Where are you?"

Violet's head cocked as she listened. She'd been in the process of dressing. With her sister's unexpected voice, Violet dropped the pale blue dress over her head.

"What's this?" Victor asked loudly. "What's this? You call only for the greater twin. I will have you know I make an excellent cocktail and since I've seen your suddenly less-precious face, I have learned to make both rum cocktails and champagne cocktails."

"What's to learn?" Isolde demanded, as Violet opened her bedroom door and watched her twin pick up their little sister, spin her in a circle, and set her down after an oomph-prompting squeeze. Victor stepped back, hands on her shoulders and looked her up and down as Isolde continued as though he hadn't greeted her with such exuberance. "You simply dump a little of this, a little of that, shake it up, and proclaim yourself a wonder."

Isolde had lost her alarmingly youthful appearance. There was a serene glow about her face. Was that because she had been spared the act of marrying the fiend Danvers? Or perhaps instead, it was because she'd finally stepped into herself?

She'd exchanged her long blonde hair for a golden bob that was all the rage. Hers was arranged into smooth waves and held down on the side with pearl hairpins. Her bright blue eyes glinted on a thinner face. Whatever had remained of her baby fat had melted away while Isolde had been traveling the world.

Violet's gaze flicked over her sister's dress with the air of a true connoisseur. Isolde had once had a wardrobe that matched the ingénue she had been, but now she looked a woman of the world. She wore a deep rose that accented her creamy skin and set off her blue eyes. Her full lips were painted a deep rose hue that matched her dress, while the rouge on her cheeks accented her healthy glow.

"You cut your hair off." Victor's voice was humour-filled and happy. "Now we can see that baby face of yours even better."

Violet peeked over Victor's back by pushing up onto her toes and setting her chin on his shoulder. "What's this? This can't be Isolde. Look at those knowing eyes. Look at that glow. Look at that sneaky tilt to her mouth. This isn't our baby sister. She's an imposter with the same face but shorter hair."

Isolde squealed, shaking off Victor and throwing herself at Violet. "Vi!"

"I think you mean, 'favourite sibling!' Don't confuse Victor. He's easily muddled."

"Being the favourite hardly counts, Vi," Tomas said from the stairs. "You're the only other girl. Isolde has to favour you. Everyone knows that."

Violet grinned at her dark-haired and dark-eyed friend. He still looked haunted, but there was an edge of happiness and peace to him despite the shell shock he struggled with. She winked at him and then turned back to Isolde.

"No, no," Victor said. "She should favour me as her older—yet not so responsible—brother. I am the one. Protector and instigator of mischief at the same time. Who else can make such wonderful claims?"

Violet was too busy squeezing her little sister tight to join in the banter. Her eyes burned with unexpected tears. "I missed you." Violet ran her hand over Isolde's head, rejoicing in the healthiness in Isolde's face, the shine in her hair, the joy in her eyes. Her sister had left cowed and a little broken and returned sure of herself, something she'd never been.

"I missed you," Isolde returned as gently. "I missed you so much. I kept thinking 'what would Violet do' over and over again. Every time I was nervous and uncertain, you saved me and you weren't even there."

Victor heard Isolde and snorted. "So you wrote a book of unaccountable value and meddled in a murder investigation?"

"Don't say those things," Tomas ordered Victor. "Isolde doesn't do that. She's the good one among you fiends."

Victor met Violet's gaze, and they winked triumphantly at each other before they faced Tomas. He'd joined them in the hallway, and the two friends threw their arms around each other and pounded one another heartily on the back. "Victor, old man, I have missed your cocktails."

"Well, they're famous now, you know? The Piccadilly Press wrote about my talents. They missed a few things, but they focused on what was important. The cocktails—"

Tomas's laugh filled the hallway, echoed by Isolde's.

"What's all this now?" the deep voice of the siblings' oldest brother demanded. "Quit hugging in the hall and order me some English tea. I have been dying a slow and miserable death without a solid tea done correctly."

"Oh my," Violet said, crossing to Gerald and kissing his cheek. "You have become Father, haven't you?"

Gerald winked at Violet and shook Victor's hand. "I am not joking about tea, sister. Please, save me. Oh, how I have suffered."

They walked down the stairs together as Violet demanded, "How was Monaco? How was Málaga? Did you love Casablanca?"

"I loved it all. I have mounds of gifts for you, darling," Isolde said happily. She moved so smoothly she seemed to be floating. Had her heart set her afloat? The happiness that radiated from Violet's little sister was like the heat of the sun, and Violet recognized it for what it was. Isolde was in love.

"What about me?" Victor gasped, holding his hand to his heart.

"Why did you appear out of nowhere? Were you supposed to be here today? I thought you were certainly supposed to be a few more days. I'd have had my Kate here if I had known."

"I cannot wait to meet this fantastical female." Isolde looked back over her shoulder, her gaze glinting at Victor. "She must be an astounding creature to be able to entrance the fickle Victor."

"Fickle? Fickle? Me? I am wounded! I am not a fickle flower. I am stalwart."

They reached the parlor, and Violet requested tea to be brought. Isolde turned in place, taking in the newly redone parlor, from the new, deep purple fabric on the Chesterfield to the paisley grey, silver, and purple curtains. "This does look nice."

"I'll take a rum cocktail," Tomas told Victor.

"It's early, isn't it?" Isolde asked, still smiling. Her gaze flicked to Tomas.

Violet's lips twitched as Tomas checked his pocket watch and then shrugged. "I suppose you're right."

Violet met Victor's gaze, and they both turned on their little sister. "It's love!" they exclaimed as one.

"I knew it would be!" Violet continued. "When is the big day, darling?"

Victor elbowed Violet. "Who cares about that, sweet sister? Do you know what this means? Lady Eleanor is getting what she always wanted, and we're saved! Isolde is marrying a respectable, well-connected, and *gloriously rich* man. Surely the woman can't hold to her rage if she's overcome by the joy of victory?"

"You'd think that, if nothing else, she would realize we engineered this duo. This is our triumph, brother. Isolde, when you tell your mother, emphasize that. It'll be harder for her to rage against us and thank us at the same time."

Tomas choked and Gerald muttered, "I told you'd they guess. You two glow. It's disgusting."

"Oh," Victor breathed, "we might be saved. We could be saved."

"No, you are still doomed," Isolde told them with a cheery smile. "Violet can't marry and have children so Geoffrey is to inherit her money."

"What's all this now?" Victor asked. "Violet wouldn't leave her money to Geoffrey. I mean, I know he's your full-brother, Isolde, but he's a devilish little wart."

"Mother has decided that you are unlikely to marry, the both of you. You're too connected at the hip, and what man would want to compete with a twin? Once she realizes you both intend to marry and forever snatch your fortunes out of her needy Geoffrey's hands...well, the only thing worse would be for Gerald to marry."

"No need to worry about that," Gerald said idly. He was examining the books on the shelf and demanded, "When did you get Greek books? Why do you have them? I know you two are cleverer than one would think, but you're not that clever. You have *La Fortuna de Los Rougon* in French? Which of you is reading novels in French?"

"Don't be silly, dear Gerald," Violet told her oldest brother.

Unlike the twins, he was a thick and hearty fellow with broad shoulders, a thinning hairline, and a little cushioning about the middle. His eyes were as kind as Isolde's and as clever as Victor's. As the heir of an earl, however, Gerald's tone and air was far more—snobbish.

Together the twins explained: "Kate."

"She's been slowly moving her books from her mother's to here," Victor said. "You'll like her, Gerald. She's brainy like you."

"Violet is brainy," Isolde protested.

"Don't defend me, darling," Violet told Isolde. "Kate really is cleverer than I."

"Vi covers it up with fluff and cocktails, darling. Kate is overtly clever."

"She can't be all that brilliant, Victor. She fell in love with you."

"Against her better judgement," Victor countered with a grin. "She knows she's drawing herself into a lifetime of nonsense. Her heart is leading her astray, and no one except her mother is trying to save her."

The twins grinned at each other, and then Victor added, "Rather like Violet's Jack. He should know better than to adore Violet. She's encumbered by so many fools that even if he realizes how clever she is, he'll still be suffocated by her hangers-on."

"She's not so clever," Gerald said, "that she didn't get caught by that newspaper woman. How did that article happen, Violet? How did you...ah...get outed?"

Vi explained that the woman who wrote the article about the twins was Jack's previous intended who wanted him back and who hated Violet from the moment they met.

"I was handicapped," Violet added, "I didn't know she existed. When I met her, dumbfounded would be an accurate description of my state of mind.'"

"Flabbergasted," Victor suggested.

"Regardless—" Violet grinned at the daily maid, who brought in the tea cart loaded with food, tea, and coffee. "I stumbled and she picked up every clue. She might be something of a fiend, but she *is* clever enough."

"She has a way with words," Gerald said, approaching the tea cart with hands rubbing together in glee. He started to load up a plate with sandwiches while Violet poured him a cup of tea and added the cream, sugar, and lemon he preferred. "I'd have winced for anyone who was the target of that diatribe. For you, love, I was quaking in my boots. Of course, I am aware of how our dear stepmother will take it."

"Ah," Violet sighed, scrunching her nose and wishing she could go back in time. The article had been published only yesterday. It was a matter of days—at most—before she was taken to account.

Gerald held up a hand. He was sipping his tea with closed eyes, breathing it in between sips.

"Surely they had tea on the steamship," Violet asked Isolde, noting that her little sister was holding hands with Tomas. "If not every place you visited—"

Vi's gaze went to her twin, landed on the held hands, and the two of them grinned. Tomas had thought himself in love with Violet since their youngest days. He had proposed more times than Violet would have wished. She loved him—like a brother. When he'd come back from the war, shell-shocked and broken, Tomas had leaned on the twins. He'd come home with waking nightmares that only the twins seemed to be able to help him with. That he'd move on and find love with Isolde had been their goal.

Violet had turned him away the final time he proposed,

confessing her love for Jack. Instead, she and Victor had suggested that Tomas spend some time in the sun with their siblings and focus on recovering. It had been the twins' expectation that Isolde, who was far better suited for him than Violet, would steal his heart. The twins might have rubbed their hands together with glee during their plotting.

"Tea tastes better in London," Gerald said, "especially after New York City. Americans don't understand the intricacies of tea and how it should be."

Violet's lips twitched as Isolde shook her head. "Heard this a few times, have you?"

"Americans have excellent coffee. They like coffee better than tea. Who can blame them?"

"I don't," Victor pronounced as he poured himself a cup of the twins' favourite Turkish coffee. "I see no reason to not have both."

"You'll come back, won't you? This eve—" Violet's question was cut off as the door to the parlor opened and their butler, Hargreaves, entered with an envelope on a tray.

"There's a wire, Mr. Victor."

Violet's brows lifted as she peeked over his shoulder. They didn't need to read the contents to know who had sent it.

"You're coming," they said together, eyeing their siblings and Tomas.

"Where?" the others asked.

"Home. We've been called home."

Isolde pressed her lips together to hide her grin as Gerald told them, "Of course you were. You're in trouble for certain."

"They don't even know we're engaged," Victor told the others. "I suspect Kate will pass muster, but Jack—with his *paid* hobby—will set Lady Eleanor to a diatribe."

"Somehow we keep forgetting to mention our engagements in our letters," Violet added.

"We should elope," Victor said, but without enthusiasm.

"Your mother-in-law will have objections to that," Violet told him.

"*I* have objections. I need the big formal event so people realize Kate really is mine. They'll keep thinking it's a joke. Especially when they meet her and realize she could have done so much better than me."

"If we're going home," Violet told the room, "we really do need to go dancing tonight. Dinner at The Savoy, dancing, and cocktails. One last moment of freedom."

"We're motoring down," Victor announced. "Drag your auto out of the garage, Tomas. If we're going to the family prison—"

"Home," Violet said.

"—we'll need an escape," Victor finished, ignoring Violet. "And an excess of gin. It's wonderful that I've just received my latest shipment of rum."

# CHAPTER TWO

"What's all this now?" Jack asked Violet, tangling his finger with hers. He'd pressed a kiss on her cheek since they had an audience of their friends and her siblings, and she snuggled a little nearer, appreciating his bulk, which made her feel infinitely better. There was something about those wide shoulders towering over Violet that felt as though he could shield her from anything. Loving him was inevitable, but she admitted that knowing he was clever, honorable, and kind made her all the more secure in his affections. His brilliant mind and penetrating gaze were always bent towards her interests, making her feel as though no one could be more treasured than she.

"Isolde, Tomas, and Gerald have returned. We've been called home. Well, Victor and I have been called home. We'll be dragging Isolde and Gerald with us. It seems that Tomas goes where Isolde goes, so he's coming too," she told him, smiling at him. She'd inserted the part about Tomas, so Jack was aware that the man who'd once thought to love Violet had thought better of it.

Vi fluttered her lashes teasingly because she knew he hated it. With a smirk and a wink, she added, "I suspect we can blame your one-time love and her clever turn of phrase for our summons. And possibly also that a zozzled Victor told our cousin, Algernon, that we were both engaged to be married."

"Algernon told your father?" Jack guessed.

Violet shrugged. "I would guess he told Uncle Kingsley who told Father. Probably in a way that was uncomfortable and embarrassing. Uncle Kingsley has never gotten over the bulk of Aunt Agatha's fortune being left to Victor and I rather than Algie. Or, preferably, himself."

"Home?" Denny glanced at his wife, Lila, and grinned lazily. "I told you they'd be called home. We can come, right? Don't say no. I am almost as excited about you getting the diatribe from the good Lady Eleanor as I was for that nonsense with dear Emily and the killers."

"Only Daniel Morgan was a killer," Violet reminded Denny, who had pulled his wife close to him and was bouncing on his toes with excitement. "The rest were only periphery."

Denny waved his hand aside—for him, the fact was of little import. "Details."

"To hear Miss Allen tell it," Lila said, wicked mischief in her gaze, "you must have been the engineer of these deaths. I heard it when I was shopping earlier today. 'Did you hear of Lady Violet? She's mad with power and manipulating would-be killers.'"

Violet laughed, but Jack grunted in irritation. "I suppose I should care more about that article."

"You will care more after Stepmother gets ahold of her. Kate!" Victor's beloved had entered the parlor. "I wondered where you were."

"Gin and Rouge found me at the door," Kate said. "I had to rub doggie bellies and tell them pretty stories." She walked across the parlor, brilliant in her emerald green evening gown, and tucked her hand into the crook of Victor's arm. He laid his hand over the top of hers as though he had always done that.

"The others are meeting us at The Savoy," Victor said. "Giles is ready with the auto. Shall we go? I am going to over-indulge before we return home and have our every move, morsel, and drink examined."

Kate gave him a baffled look, asking Violet, "It can't be that bad, can it?"

"Oh, it is!" Denny chuckled and rubbed his hands together. "Let's go. I'm starving. Lila won't let me just eat and nap. She made me walk with her today, and then I had to eat a salad and soup. Salad! Greens! Not a single steak or piece of ham. I may faint if we don't hurry."

"You're fat, love," Lila told Denny. "Your buttons are straining and you may just split your pants while we dance."

Violet choked on her laughter, and Jack had to rub his hand up and down her back to help her catch her breath. Or maybe he only took the opportunity to do so. She grinned at the idea as he asked, "Are you going to tell them we're engaged?"

"I already told the people who matter, darling," Violet answered. "You asked Father for his blessing, which he gave. I suspect the only one who doesn't know is Stepmother because not even Father wants to hear the diatribe and not even Father can silence her."

~

"Violet," Victor said, in between dances. He set aside his potted shrimps on the nearest table and downed his cocktail. There was something in his tone that drew her attention. Something was wrong. Her gaze narrowed on him.

The club was crowded with bodies while one of the most gorgeous women Violet had ever seen wailed her song over the sound of dancing. She had to step close to him to hear what he was saying.

It was so hot in the club that she had only water with ice, and she downed it in one mighty go before she addressed her brother. "Did you lose Kate? What's wrong?"

"She's in the powder room, following some piece of Algie's."

Violet's brows lifted. "Piece? Women aren't pieces, you fiend."

"*Sleuthing*," Victor added, with emphasis to demand she focus on what he thought mattered. "Kate's been around you too much, my love."

"Sleuthing about what?"

Victor glanced around for Jack, saw him at the bar, and said, "Darling one, Stepmother is having a house party while we're there."

"Oh?" Trepidation ran down Vi's spine.

"It seems the invite to this party was for some well-connected lads. Handsome young fellows who are, perhaps, willing to strap on a ball and chain."

"For Isolde?" Violet asked, even though she knew it wasn't correct.

"No," Victor said, stepping back as Violet's face flushed with rage.

"She might not know that we're engaged," Violet told him, referring to her stepmother, smacking his shoulder even though it wasn't his fault, "but she is well aware that I have no interest in other men."

"An oversight," he suggested, but they knew it wasn't so. Lady Eleanor was going to throw well-connected and probably destitute men at Violet until the stubborn woman saw the light. Even then, she'd probably do the equivalent of commenting on the nice night and refusing to admit the sun was high overhead—or in other words, Lady Eleanor wouldn't acknowledge Violet's engagement until Violet had a babe in arms and an updated will. What Violet didn't understand was *why* Lady Eleanor wanted Violet to throw Jack over for one of these men.

Jack returned with a cocktail for Violet. "I asked the barman like you requested, and he suggested this. It's a French75." Jack handed Violet a sort of creamy yellow drink with a curl of lemon peel in it, and Violet took it with glee.

Vi grinned at him and tried to hide her rage. He was too aware of her, and she felt his gaze flicking over her face as strongly as a caress, but she avoided meeting his eyes and sniffed the drink. "Ooh, lemon?"

Jack nodded. Of course it was lemon, it had a lemon peel. She was just trying to distract him.

She took a sip and paused. She let the drink set in her mouth as her gaze fixed on her cousin, Algernon, who sneered. He was beyond Jack's shoulder and looking her over. Violet glanced at Victor, jerking her gaze to Algie, and Victor followed her eyes. Behind Algie was his too-often companion, Theodophilus. He'd once cornered Violet and left her bruised, a circumstance that Victor had already repeatedly made Theo pay for.

Victor's head tilted, and Theodophilus flushed, but he lifted a challenging brow.

"Excuse me." Victor handed Violet his cocktail.

"Don't get arrested," Violet told him.

"What's this now?" Jack demanded. Violet placed her hand on his arm, holding him to her as Victor stepped away.

"Don't worry your pretty little head about it," she said. "If Victor gets arrested, it'll matter far less than if you do, my lad."

They watched as Victor crossed the room, grabbed Theodophilus by the lapels, and dragged him out of the club.

"Oh," Isolde said, approaching on Tomas's arm. Her gaze followed the lion version of Victor. "Who is that? My goodness, did he do something to Kate? Victor does look fierce, doesn't he?"

"Not to Kate," Jack ground out, as Violet held him even tighter.

"Don't worry your pretty little heads about it," Violet told them all.

Tomas snorted. "I'll just follow Victor and see if he needs a hand."

Violet clung tighter to Jack when he tried to join them and whispered, "Why don't you let them do this part?"

"It's my job now," Jack growled, wrapping his arm around her waist.

"Jack, you work with Scotland Yard."

"It's my job to protect you," he muttered.

"But you love detecting," Violet told him, dropping her voice low as Kate rejoined them. "You don't want to cause trouble at the Yard."

"Victor stepped outside," Violet told Kate vaguely, waggling her brows so Kate would know something was up. Handing Kate Victor's drink, Violet suggested, "Perhaps we should go home for quiet drinks after we gather up Victor."

Jack's gaze flicked to Violet. "I'll get a black cab."

Violet grabbed at him, but he escaped her.

"Will he pound that fellow?" Isolde asked. "Bloody him up a bit? Perhaps get the boys thrown into the slammer?"

Violet shot Isolde a glare, which made her drop her expression to a smooth compliance with only a sparkle in her gaze to admit to mischief.

With the gents all gone except for Gerald, who was dancing with a slim, ginger girl, Algernon approached.

"What's all this is, now?" Algie asked.

"What *is* all this?" Violet demanded, eyeing Algie like the worm he was.

"I didn't come with him, Vi. He hunted me up. He's been following me around like a street dog. Vi..." Algie glanced around. "He's well-connected. I've been debating...um...trying to find a way to warn you."

Violet's gaze narrowed. "She didn't." Violet didn't need him to nod to know that her stepmother had, in fact, invited one of the few men who'd made Violet truly afraid. Her heart skipped a beat, and she would have stumbled if she weren't standing still.

"She did," Algie said. "I overheard it. I didn't think Theo would have told me. We aren't friendly these days. He was prosing on about how..."

Violet heart was racing, and her vision had narrowed down only to his face. Her home.

"He's leaving tomorrow." Algie blushed and gazed at the ground. "Well he *was*. They expect you to come around then too. There's a semi-open invite for Theo and a few others from what I've heard."

Violet laid her hand on his arm for balance as she breathed slowly in and hooted out a breath. It wasn't helping. She wanted Jack. Blindly, Violet turned to the exit.

"Violet," Algie added, "all your stepmother wants is well-connection in who you marry. And preferably idle, like the aristocrats of the last few generations. She cares little about anything beyond that. I know you know her, but...be careful. Some of those gents she invited are— Well, I wouldn't want my sister *or* my cousin around them."

Violet nodded without looking back and made her way to Jack and Victor. She found the three of her boys in the alleyway near the entrance, smoking cigarettes. Violet walked straight up to Jack and wrapped her arms around his waist.

She didn't say anything, but she felt him tense since her actions were totally out of normal behavior for her.

"What's wrong?" Victor demanded.

"Mother invited that fellow you just, ah—educated—to the house."

"What's this now?" Victor's voice was a cool, low threat.

Violet simply pressed her face into Jack's chest and breathed in. She'd faced more lately than Theodophilus Smythe-Hill, but he'd been one of the first to teach her how much physically weaker women were than men.

"No," Victor said. "Tomas?"

Violet let Jack warm her while her brother went to re-bruise his knuckles against Theodophilus Smythe-Hill's face.

# CHAPTER THREE

The earl's house was one of those brick and stone monstrosities that had been handed down from the dawn of forever ago through the generations to the current day. Violet was sure that *someone* knew when the Carlyles built it or took possession or however owning this beast came about, but she wasn't that person.

Unlike Gerald, Isolde, and Geoffrey, the twins had been raised mostly by their great-aunt from their mother's side of the family. Both of the twins could still channel their aristocratic ancestry and pull out generations of self-righteous, self-important sneering when they needed to get their way. Despite that, they hadn't spent all that much time under the hallowed roof.

In the simplest of descriptions, the house was a rectangle. To be fair, it was *huge*. You could get lost in the beast and Violet intended to do so. Soon enough, her stepmother would call Violet down to the carpet, and the sheer fact that the woman was inviting snakes like Theodophilus to the house at the same time as Violet and Isolde was reason enough to delay torment.

Outside of the house, in the center of the rectangle, was a grand staircase that led up to doors big enough to ride a horse through. Violet would enjoy her family a lot more if they *did* ride horses through the house. Lady Eleanor, however, acted as though she had a board strapped to her spine and a stick in other places. Perhaps when Gerald was the earl the family would loosen up.

The rolling acres that led up to the house were sculpted and manicured within an inch of their lives, making sure that even the trees knew that they were aristocratic. The hedges were upright and green, not daring to have a twig out of place. The large pots of flowers were lush and abundant. Anything else would be unacceptable.

There was a fountain in the center of a circular roundabout that was probably stolen from some Roman villa. Perhaps a more upright ancestor had commissioned the thing. The statue was all muscular back and flexing arms with strong, tensed legs. Atlas was holding up the world under the spray of water. Violet glanced at it, taking in the statue so large it matched the size of the house. As always, she appreciated the beauty of the flexed muscles and wondered if her love of Jack's stature came from a lifetime of this kind of art. A question for when Victor wasn't in the auto.

Violet smirked at the thought. Victor and Violet might be reflections of each other, the opposite sides of the same coin with matching coloring, sharp features, and slender builds, but he was her brother and he did *not* want to know why she appreciated Jack's form.

Which meant, of course, that Violet should have to tell him when he least expected it. Yes, that was the best course. She'd find her chance while they were home and hopefully in view of the statue.

"Are you going to tell her?" Jack asked, his voice low.

Violet pressed herself against his side and looked up at him through her lashes. He was a handsome man. Though sometimes she wondered if he really was or if she was just blinded by her love. To her, however, he was the most attractive man she had ever seen.

"Yes, of course," Violet said, hoping for a cheery tone and noting it came out more as flinching.

"If we're actually going to wed, Violet darling, you will have to tell her, or we'll have to elope and reveal it afterwards."

Violet laid her head on his shoulder, staring at the house and knowing they should get out of the auto. As she watched, her father's butler, Smalley, opened the door to the house, stepping back and letting her father exit. "Of course we're getting married."

Father looked like the country earl he was. He had a pipe hanging from his mouth and a brown suit that was a bit rumpled but very nice all the same. He stopped at the top of the steps and cocked his head as he examined the auto that was not dispensing his children.

Violet grinned. He was utterly unruffled that they were lingering in the auto rather than rushing up to lavish him with love.

"It's not that I don't want everyone to know," Violet said as Victor's man, Giles, finally opened Victor's side of the auto. "It's that I don't want her to ruin my happiness. I am proud to be engaged to you, Jack, and I will be proud to be your wife. I just wanted to...savor...all of this. She'll ruin it. She'll make it into a fight."

Denny had driven his own auto, a Silver Ghost, and he had already handed Lila out of the vehicle. They wandered over to look into Victor's auto, bending down to smirk through the window. Denny opened the door, happily demanding, "Come on now. Don't cower. Buck up. What did those Americans say? Pull yourself up by your bootstraps, kids."

Violet's lips twitched, but Jack said, "I suppose we can't hide forever." With that statement, Jack stepped from the auto.

"Let's run away," Violet suggested as Jack held out his hand for Violet.

"You'll have to face her sooner or later, Violet. She's married to your father."

Denny's evil laugh serenaded Violet stepping out and smoothing her dress. "You know her well, old man. Word to the wise: never refer to Lady Eleanor as Vi's mother."

"My mother was Penelope Allyn-Carlyle. If we are talking about second mothers, that role was filled by Aunt Agatha when Lady Eleanor declined it. This woman is only married to Father."

Her father started down the steps as Violet placed her hand on Jack's arm. As Father reached the bottom, Lady Eleanor came outside. Unlike Father, Violet's stepmother did not bother to descend the steps. "What *is* taking so long?"

"Just stretching a bit, Lady Eleanor." Victor had tucked Kate under his arm, and they'd turned to watch the countess flash with anger. She despised that the twins refused to call her Mother.

"Father," Violet said, kissing his cheek without letting go of Jack. "You remember Jack, of course, as well as Denny and Lila."

"Of course I do," Father said. He accepted Violet's kiss with a snuffle. "You said you were bringing three more. Where are they? Who are they? We have quite a full house. Your mother invited Sir Rosens, son, and daughter. Oh, and Bennet Nelson's sons. Some other fellow who hasn't bothered to show or send his regrets. If I'd known we were going to be swimming in guests, I'd have delayed asking you to come home. Let alone with Devonsly here as well. The most that can be said of him is that he carries cigars. The man's an out and out fool, and I don't care if our families are linked back to time immemorial."

Violet's brows lifted. She hid her satisfaction that Father, at least, was not involved in the plot to oust Jack and replace him with some well-born beggar. "You'll be delighted to know, Father, that our extra guests are a surprise. It's Gerald, Isolde, and our friend, St. Marks. They've come home."

Her father turned to his wife. "Isolde's home, darling. Since Geoffrey's been sent down already, we'll have the children home at once. Don't think that's happened in many a year."

Lady Eleanor's narrowed gaze transformed into actual joy. Violet, on the other hand, smoothed her reaction to an even expression. Having them all together hadn't happened because when the others were home, the twins had been sent to Aunt Agatha. Violet's dead brothers were more strangers than mentors, and her memories of them were few.

Violet wondered just what Geoffrey had done to get sent down from school so early in the year. How old was he now? Violet glanced at Isolde who had just turned twenty years old. That must make Geoffrey about sixteen years old.

"What good luck for you, love," Father said under his breath. "She's been practicing her lecture. Maybe Isolde coming back with that rich friend of yours will distract her. She's a dog with a bone about the fortune you inherited. As if I have any power of it or you. Not like Agatha left it to me. She knew you didn't need a keeper. Your mother shouldn't have foisted you off on other people if she wanted influence with you." He shook his head as Violet hid her reaction at Lady Eleanor being called her mother. "I told her she reaped what she sowed when she told me of this party of hers," he continued. "As if you're going to throw your Jack over for one of these poor fools. Ellie stopped speaking to me until the guests arrived. By Jove, girl, marry the fellow, travel for a while, and maybe she'll give me a little peace."

Violet gasped while Victor laughed evilly. Denny glanced between the two of them and then grinned so widely at his wife that she elbowed him.

"I knew this would be absolutely fabulous," he whispered so loudly that even Lady Eleanor from her place at the top of the stairs heard him.

Thankfully, Violet thought, Stepmother hadn't heard Father. Violet wasn't sure her father had ever been more rebellious.

Denny continued, little caring that everyone heard him. "This is going to be almost as good as when we went home and found Martha had engaged herself to that traveling salesman."

"Contain yourself, my lad," Lila told him. "You'll give yourself a brain fever."

Before they reached the top of the steps, Tomas's auto arrived with the maids, Isolde, and Gerald. He leapt out of the car, revealing how much better he was feeling. A mere moment later, Tomas handed out Isolde and Gerald followed.

"That is how you exit an auto," Lady Eleanor said to the twins. "Lingering is rude."

"Ah," Victor said in a snide tone but neither of the twins replied. Lady Eleanor didn't even acknowledge Kate or Jack, let alone Lila and Denny, when she called, "Isolde!"

Reaching out her hands, their stepmother darted down the stairs.

"I can see why you don't call her Mother," Denny said under his breath. "Rather a different reception, isn't it? Let alone how she snubbed my lovely self."

"Don't worry, laddie," Violet told Denny, "and quit feeling bad for little Violet and Victor. I assure you that, although Aunt Agatha didn't throw herself down the stairs or weep at our arrival, she made sure we knew she was happy to see us."

"I always liked Aunt Agatha, Vi." Denny's defense of the child-Violet made her pat him on the cheek.

"You've a good heart under all that chocolate and gin, Denny. Who's ready to see the lads Lady Eleanor brought in for me?"

"Let's have them strut around like horses at Tattersalls," Denny suggested. "Put them through their paces, so to speak, before letting them down hard and vicious. Never appreciated a fortune hunter. Female or male, quite ruins one's faith in humanity."

"That does sound like fun," Victor said. "Seeing as how you and I would get to sit back and watch."

"Bit like a good opera," Denny said, rubbing his hands together, "without the caterwauling."

Victor snorted. "No doubt, Violet will sink into one of those books she's the greater writer of and avoid the boys. We'll have to draw her out, so to speak. Drag her in for the performances before she fictionally murders them all. Seeing as how I only...ah...help to a lesser extent with our invaluable fiction."

"Not invaluable," Violet corrected. "Fiction of unaccountable value. Quite different, lesser twin."

Kate grinned at Violet with a sneaky wink before speaking smoothly to Victor. "Miss Allen only made you the lesser twin in that article because she knew you'd quote it. I'm certain she took your measure. Tell the truth. You love being the lesser twin."

"She took all of our measures," Victor said.

"Leave Violet be," Kate suggested, squeezing his arm. "You wouldn't love it if my mother brought around more-approved lads to sway me from you. Jack doesn't care for it, and Violet doesn't want to be the symbol of money bags for hard-pressed lads."

"But it's fun," Victor whined.

"Look," Denny told Lila, "Kate saw how well Isolde has Tomas in hand and realized she'd fallen behind the young 'uns." He whispered with a conspiratorial tone in that too-loud voice. "I'm still excited to see Lady Eleanor go on the attack. I *do* hope she'll go after Jack. If she does, our fun won't be ruined even if Victor and Jack oust the money grubbers."

They turned as one to see if anyone heard them, but Lady Eleanor and the earl were encompassed with the other children. They all watched Father and Gerald shake hands and Isolde press a kiss on their father's cheek.

Lila glanced at the others before turning back to the scene of the happy family. "Denny was almost poetic on the road. I felt certain he'd break into a sonnet at any moment, but it turns out he was only discussing your torment and not a fresh box of Belgium chocolate."

"You wound me, wife."

"One can only hope," she shot back, winking at Violet. "You know Vi is my favourite."

## CHAPTER FOUR

"Those boys are intended for you," Victor told Violet with a little glee.

The twins were standing together on the balcony they shared between their bedrooms. Lady Eleanor had tried to separate them once upon a time, but the twins had taught her the error of her ways. Since then they had neighboring rooms with the balcony, so Lady Eleanor could pretend they'd gone to bed like good children when really they were flitting in between each other's rooms with the balcony as their highway.

"They're all youngish and well-connected. If Theo makes it, he, at least, could claim handsome. Well..." Victor grinned evilly. "He'd have been able to before his recent mishap. But Devonsly does look like he got hit with a brick in his formative years, and the younger of those Nelson brothers is so homely, it's remarkable."

Violet glanced up at him and then away. They watched as, below them, Lord Devonsly said something to the other three men. Between both Bennet Nelson's sons, Lord Devonsly of the bankrupt estate, and Sir Maxwell Rosens's son, Lady Eleanor had provided Violet four options to Jack. If you included that one-time bruiser of arms, Theo, she'd have scored well for the five most unpalatable of hard-up men England had to offer.

"As opposed to the rich, but not rich enough, Jack Wakefield." Violet's feeling on the matter was clear with her snarl. "Why Lady Eleanor thinks she gets to vote or be involved in any way, I have no idea. Even if I wasn't in love with Jack, I'd never, ever consider one of these fellows."

"There, there." Victor's voice had too much humour for Violet to believe that false attempt at soothing.

Violet turned, leaning her back against the balustrade. "I suppose I shouldn't be surprised."

"I think the only thing that surprised me," her twin admitted, "is that we didn't expect and prepare for it. If Algie hadn't clued us in, we'd have been caught entirely blind-sided. Who knew we could be grateful to the wart?" Victor joined her in leaning with his legs crossed at the ankle as hers were. "Thank goodness Ginny is at school and not here to witness both Lady Eleanor's nature and our idiocy."

"We're fools," Violet agreed, running her fingers through her bob. It was time to get her hair trimmed again. If only her life were so simple as to whether her hair was how she wanted it and the trauma of her new shoes pinching her feet.

"You'll have to cling to Jack like glue. Him or me. They'll be throwing themselves at you. You're the golden calf, love. Whatever it takes—"

"Well," Violet told him with a bit of a smile, "I am delightful."

"You're rich, love. *And* clever. If they're smart enough to want that."

Jack and Kate appeared on the edge of the balcony from Victor's bedroom. Their heads were tilted to the same angle as they examined the twins.

"I suppose we'll have to get used to finding them like this." Kate's smile faded when she saw who was in the garden below.

"I suppose so." Jack didn't sound as though he minded finding the twins together, but his expression turned cold as he followed Kate's gaze past the twins.

Victor held out his hand to Kate and she crossed to him, tangling their fingers together. Victor pressed a kiss on the top of Kate's head. "Tell her, my love."

Kate grinned at Violet. "What am I telling her?" she asked.

"She's rich."

"You're rich, Vi," Kate said immediately, her eyes glinting with humour.

"Are we stating random facts?" Jack took the spot next to Violet. "You're beautiful, Vi."

Violet chuckled under her breath while Victor moaned.

"Below us," Victor said as though conducting a tour, "Lord Devonsly. I assume he's favoured because of the title. Near-bankrupt but nice enough. Went to school with him. He's excellent at cricket. Beside him you'll see the two Nelson sons. Not broke, but they'll eventually have to find work. They've avoided it thus far. There was once some connections between the wealthy Wanda Greene and both lads, but it all came to naught."

"Uh-oh," Kate said. "Having lost one heiress in the wild, they'll be all the more determined to acquire the one in semi-captivity."

"Indeed." Victor wrapped his arm around Kate's shoulders. "Your mind is a wonder."

"And the other?"

"Mrs. Rosens is a crony of our stepmother. Her second son isn't exactly a pauper, but he'd be approved simply for not being you, Jack. He's also not swimming in money like Violet. I'm sure he'd like to paddle through the bouillon with the belle of our ball."

Jack's face was still, even and cold. He stared down at the four men. "They've seen us," he told the other three, who had turned their backs on the garden. "Shall I look demonic? Take them aside and threaten the lads? Put on a dog-in-the-manger attitude?"

Violet's lips twitched. "Alas, I fear we will further drive Stepmother mad no matter what we do. I think it should be Victor and I who torment the interlopers since we should like Stepmother to eventually —well, she'll never love you."

Jack pressed his hand over his heart, but his cold smile told Violet exactly how much he minded.

"While discussing facts," Violet mused, "we should have discussed our stupidity and lack of foresight. Mine and Victor's of course. You two are excused for not having spent the entirety of your life dealing with these..."

"Shenanigans," Victor filled in.

Violet shook her head.

"Manipulations?" Kate suggested, leaning her head on Victor's shoulder. "I find I am quite grateful that she's not as angry with you. I am utterly terrified of her."

"Well, love, I suspect she's reserving judgement. They say you're clever, don't you know? Lady Eleanor is probably grateful you aren't a dancer."

Violet's snort of laughter made her choke, and she leaned over, coughing into her hand before she straightened. "Oh, dear. This will be an adventure."

"We should recover in Cuba," Victor declared. "I know I just got a restock of my rum, but I could stand buying some in person."

"No," Jack said. "We're not running. We visit. We leave. We go back about our lives. If we run, she'll think she can keep manipulating things. She'll think she scared us off."

Victor gasped, holding a hand to his chest and fluttering his lashes at Jack. "You, sir! You, sir, are brainy indeed. It's...it's...I feel as though I could light my cigarette off the flames of your wit."

"Stop it," Kate told him, elbowing him lightly in the side.

Victor immediately cleared his throat. "Anything for you, love." He glanced at Violet. "After seeing how well Isolde has Tomas trained, I thought I had better obey better until after I've got Kate lassoed with the old ball and chain."

"You're mixing your metaphors," Kate told him. "Though, I suppose you know that since you did it on purpose."

"Indeed," Victor said. "Darling Vi, we must start our new story while we're here. No longer are we the secret V.V. Twinnings. If we're going to keep writing our unaccountable nonsense, we are going to do it with bells on. I was thinking of a short piece about an earl who marries and whose wife—the villainess—tries to murder his children."

"Seems just the thing," Violet said with a rare seriousness.

"Let's go meet them," Kate said. "I promised Denny we'd knock on his door before we go down. He says watching Violet be cornered by money grubbers is worth the cost of his nap, but he may snooze through any and all activities to make up for it."

Violet glanced down at her wrinkled travel dress and said, "I'll just change and meet you in the hall, shall I?"

~

Denny had the sort of glee-filled expression that only seemed to cross his face when Lila was wearing something particularly scandalous or when he opened a new box of chocolates. Violet took one look at him, hooked her arm through Lila's, and said, "I think we should move ahead before I accidentally push your beloved down the stairs."

Lila patted Violet's hand. "It's hard being the fox, darling. You're so good at being the hound. Especially since people look at you and see a rabbit."

"There are too many animals in that statement," Violet said. "I feel certain that we should be visiting a menagerie rather than wandering the house a bit before we dress for dinner. Let's hurry before Jack and Victor step out and try to be protective."

They moved ahead with Denny following closely behind so as not to, "miss any of the dramatic portrayals."

Violet was looking back at Denny, scowling, when someone said, "Lady Vi," with a charming, deep voice.

Violet tensed, and Lila squeezed her hand. Together they turned with Denny giggling like a drunkard behind them.

"Hello there. May I make myself known to you? I am Leopold Nelson." The grin was wide and a bit snake-like. The way his eyes raked over her told Violet that he had come for the money but her looks would make do. He seemed ready to disconnect his jaw and swallow her whole. She tried for a charming smile but was certain she failed miserably.

"Get your head in the game, Vi," Denny whispered in his mocking tone that carried across the entirety of the house.

Violet gave Denny a chilling expression that promised retribution.

She didn't hold out her hand to Leopold, but she did slap on enough of a smile to pass muster and introduced Lila and Denny.

"Pleasure," Denny said, shaking Leopold Nelson's hand enthusiastically. "I'm just *so* glad you're here. It's a true joy. Just a true joy." Denny's grin was so infectious that Leopold Nelson was smiling back with trepidation in his gaze, wondering why Denny was so happy to see him.

"And this is your wife?" Leopold asked. It was clear he was ensuring that Denny had no claims on Violet.

Denny laughed outright and nodded.

"You're acting a fool, lad," Lila told her husband lazily. "We've come down with Victor, along with other friends—Kate Lancaster and Jack Wakefield. We're all good friends—" Lila shot Violet an apologetic look before she clarified, "of Victor. Violet too, of course, but of Victor."

Violet pressed her lips tightly together as she saw the gleam of satisfaction in Leopold Nelson's gaze. Her betraying, horrible, soon-to-be revenged upon friends had lumped Jack with Victor to give these fortune hunters hopes.

"I love you, wife!" Denny told her in his stage-whisper.

She grinned at him, winked, and using his same too-loud whisper said, "Happy Anniversary, darling."

Violet unlinked herself from Lila, her gaze caught by a young man in the doorway of the billiards room. It took her a moment to recognize the sallow lad as her brother, Geoffrey.

"Excuse me," Violet told the others, leaving before they could stop her and moving towards her little brother. She couldn't remember when she'd last seen the boy, and what memories she had weren't fond, but he was her brother. There had been a time, Vi reminded herself, when she hadn't been that large of a fan of Isolde as well.

# CHAPTER FIVE

Geoffrey looked a lot like Isolde. On their sister, the bone structure, full lips, and coloring looked quite healthy. On Geoffrey, it looked like he desperately needed a day in the sun. His lips looked as though he'd had some sort of reaction to a faulty lipstick. They were too red and too big. But mostly, Violet thought, it was the turn to his expression. Had he always been so sour? He puckered like someone had shoved a lemon in his mouth and he still hadn't gotten the flavour out.

"Hullo there," Violet said to him, cocking her head. "Been a while."

"If it isn't V.V. Twinnings," Geoffrey said snidely. His gaze flit over her with so much derision that Violet thought she could feel it.

"If it isn't a lad who should be at school," Violet countered. She let him see the corresponding sourness in her expression even though she had a decade on him. "Sent down already? Is it a new record? Didn't the term just start?"

"I got teased about you," he said rudely, giving her the side-eye without even trying to hide it. "I took care of the loudmouths, but it ended with me being sent home. *Disgraced earl's child.*" His tone, quoting the article, was vicious and dark.

Violet lifted a brow and then looked beyond him, noting that he'd been playing billiards with the other Nelson brother. The younger brother was standing in the shadows of the room, watching their interaction with interest.

"Me?" Violet laughed. She had to hold a hand to her side, laughing so hard it hurt. "Oh boyo—" Violet shook her head, nodded to the Nelson brother who was about one step from taking notes on their interaction. "Don't be a wart."

"Mother says to be nice to you so you'll put me in your will. I'm not sure I will. I'm not sure licking your feet is worth that."

"It's not." Violet's gaze narrowed on him, and he met her gaze in challenge. "My will has all the money going to charities. They're far less likely to kill a girl."

Geoffrey paled. "That's not true, is it?"

"Indeed," Violet lied.

Currently all of her money was split evenly between Isolde and Victor. Their oldest brother, Gerald, didn't need anything as he was getting the majority of the family coffers. Isolde and Victor didn't need anything either, as they were all receiving *something* from Father, and Victor had inherited from Aunt Agatha as well. Violet had little concern that her heirs would kill her for the money. She suddenly realized she wouldn't have the same faith in young Geoffrey and sadness rushed her.

"Not all of it," Violet told him. "I did leave some to care for my dog, though I suppose I can count on Victor for that, but what if we die at the same time? Sweet Rouge is a girl's best friend, you know. One must take care of one's dependents. Oh, and my maid. Beatrice is my angel."

"You left money for your dog but not for me?" Geoffrey gasped. His too-pale skin flushed in a mottled fashion, leaving him blotchy. Given his paleness, he looked as though he might have caught something terrible. Scarlet fever or the measles. "Your maid?"

"I did indeed." Violet winked at him and then left the billiards room before she said something that would ruin any relationship they would ever have. She reminded herself that she adored Isolde these days, and for a while there, Violet had been unsure of her.

She supposed she should have introduced herself to the fellow in the corner, but he'd been happy enough lurking and listening. Violet slid out the doorway sideways to avoid the Nelson brother who'd introduced himself and escaped outside. She had expected Jack, Victor, and Kate to appear by now, but they were nowhere to be seen.

Violet glanced around like she was going to break into a house or out of a jail before she hurried down the hallway and darted into the kitchens. Violet found the housekeeper and Cook together as she often had in the past.

"My darlings!" Violet said, holding out her arms. "How I have missed you."

Cook looked up at Violet over a table of bread dough, and Mrs. Jones, the housekeeper, shot Violet a quelling look.

"What's all this? Where is the shout of joy? Did you not realize that we've come bearing gifts?"

"You usually do," Cook said with that dry voice. "Chocolate and alcohol. A little of the green would be welcome. You inherited loads of money. Buy a house on the sea and hire me and Margaret."

Violet grinned. "Father would have a grudge then."

"I'm not leaving," Mrs. Jones replied. "When I move to a cottage by the sea, I won't be working."

"You'd never take Victor or me seriously anyway."

Vi really had spent too much time with the servants as a girl. It wasn't because they weren't great, although they were. It was because Violet had hated her stepmother, and spending time with anyone else was delightful in comparison. Somewhere during her childhood, Mrs. Jones and Cook had become two of Violet's favourite people.

They chatted for a while before Vi asked, "How long have they been here?"

The housekeeper glanced at Violet, at Cook, then cleared her throat. "Lady Eleanor suggested you might arrive a few days ago. I think she expected you'd come straight down when the wire was sent."

Violet laughed, loving that idea. They'd delayed on purpose, gone shopping, attended a play or two. "How bad are the interlopers?"

"Devonsly isn't so bad. A bit spoiled, like all of you are." There was a very telling silence after that statement that had Violet lifting her brows. Neither of the women said another word.

Violet gave the women a small smile. "None more so than young Geoffrey. Has he always been such a devilish wart?"

Cook crowed, but the housekeeper, Mrs. Jones, didn't reply. Violet smirked at them and then added, "You know they're here for my money."

"Or something," Mrs. Jones muttered ominously.

Violet watched Mrs. Jones, but the woman simply pursed her mouth, adjusted her apron, and avoided Violet's gaze. "Interesting."

Cook snorted, digging her hands into the dough she was forming.

Violet winked at Cook, who glanced at the housekeeper and said, "You'd be wiser to choose a different fellow if you're determined to get married."

"I am," Violet said. "The money grubbers are not, however, the one I will marry."

"One?" Cook demanded. "Is there *a* one?"

"Mmm. Yes. It seems I forgot to explain to my stepmother that I've already promised myself to another."

Mrs. Jones closed her eyes as she took a deep breath. Violet bit the inside of her mouth to hold back a laugh at the expression. Drama was definitely going to ensue, and poor Mrs. Jones would experience all Lady Eleanor's feelings on the subject.

"The detective?" Cook asked. "We've heard some thoughts about that man."

"Her business is no business of ours." Mrs. Jones had the smooth servant's expression on again, which Violet very rarely saw.

Cook glanced at the housekeeper and pursed her lips. "You should turn your eye on the gardens. When everyone goes up to dress for dinner, you might find something interesting."

Violet's brows lifted, and she nodded once. "That's rather soon, isn't it?" The wicked glance Violet and Cook exchanged made Mrs. Jones sigh.

"You should stay out of it, Helena," Mrs. Jones said to Cook.

"I'm not going to stand by and watch her ruin her life," Cook shot back. "She's our girl."

Mrs. Jones glanced at Violet. "I don't want her to be unhappy either. Have a little faith in Lady Violet. She's never been stupid. We'd have to worry if this circus was for one of the younger ones."

Cook glanced at Violet, who had cocked her head as she examined Mrs. Jones.

"You need to be careful." Violet grinned at the duo of servants who she'd known the entirety of her life. "It's a tricky thing to work here."

She didn't expand on working for Lady Eleanor. Both Mrs. Jones and Cook had worked for the earl long before he'd married Lady Eleanor. Given what Violet knew of her stepmother, Vi expected the transition had been rough.

"I *am* aching for a walk." Violet looked up at a sound in the doorway and saw Isolde.

"You are in trouble with Victor and Jack for leaving them with your lads. Jack was...ah...displeased."

"My lads?" Violet's lip twitched. "I'm certain they're not mine."

Isolde glanced at Violet and then kissed Mrs. Jones and Cook on the cheek even though they tried to swat her away.

"Shouldn't they be roasting the fatted calf for you?" Violet asked Isolde, lips twitching. "How did you escape your mother, oh belovedest one? Though...really, excuse me. That title does go to yon young wart, Geoffrey."

Isolde rubbed her hands together. "I have my ways."

It was notable, Violet thought, that Isolde didn't defend Geoffrey. Of all the siblings, Isolde knew Geoffrey best. Violet glanced at Isolde, at the others, and said, "It *is* almost time to dress for dinner."

Isolde only nodded, recognizing the certain something in Violet's tone. "What are you up to?"

"Who me?" Violet winked and walked out the kitchen door to the back gardens. She glanced around, searching for Jack and Victor. Neither of them would welcome her sneaking around without them, and Violet was curious about just what she was supposed to be seeing in the gardens.

If Cook sent her out there, it must be something that was at least moderately scandalous. Violet had always liked the somewhat salacious twinkle in Cook's eyes. She was a woman who caught the littlest of details and put them together into a picture that few would see.

Violet caught movement near the kitchen garden by the hedges. She considered for a moment and then decided to approach from the side. She took the gardener's route through the kitchen garden, tiptoeing as carefully as possible. With the skitter of pebbles, Violet was certain she'd never have a future in hunting.

This portion of the gardens was more functional than decorative, with the last of the summer vegetables coming in. She sniffed, biting her lips and stepping from the path into the garden beds. Her heels sunk into the soft loam, but she heard a girl say, "How long?"

The man's voice was not pleading, but more quietly commanding. "Don't be like that, love."

Vi scowled. She immediately didn't like him just for the way he was speaking. Was one of *her* lads stepping out on her? She grinned in anticipation of telling her stepmother. Between the one using the family abode to conduct his romance and the one who had previously left her bruised, Lady Eleanor had picked some real money-grubbing winners.

"I'll be any way I like," the girl hissed back. "You keep making promises, but you don't follow through. Why should I keep listening to you?"

Violet silently cheered for the girl. This lad was a real rotten tomato.

"Enough," he snapped in that low, commanding voice. It was like he was pretending to be a lover but failing miserably.

Violet sniffed, then caught Jack's gaze. He was watching her from the corner of the garden, hands on his hips. Vi placed a finger over her lips and then waved him over. He crossed, but Violet turned back to the hedge that was hiding her, ear tilted towards the couple on the other side.

"Enough?" the girl demanded. "Enough what? Enough of your empty promises? Enough of your lies? Enough of all of it!" There was the sound of a small struggle and then the girl said, "Stop it."

Jack placed his hand on Violet's back, and she jumped even though she'd been expecting him. She was tempted to go save the girl on the other side of the hedges, but she wanted to hear was happening. She'd step in if things escalated further.

"What," he breathed into her ear, "do you think you're doing?"

She turned and placed her finger over his lips.

"I said to stop it," the girl said again. "I'm not going to keep playing this game with you."

Violet's eyes widened at Jack. She was sure he could see the combination of fury and glee in them. Was it so wrong that Violet was glad Lady Eleanor had chosen so badly? Vi did feel bad, however, for the girl. That was a girl whose heart was involved with a right bastard.

Whatever had happened between the couple had come to an end, and Violet was left alone with Jack. "Hello, love." Her merry grin wasn't returned. She tried winking but he wasn't moved. "So you're angry then?"

He shook his head. "No." He didn't smile, but she could see the humour in his eyes and the twitch at the corner of his mouth.

"What are you, then?"

"Violet—" Jack had that worried look that told her he was remembering how many times she'd been hurt while interfering in things like this.

"I was only curious which one of my lads was stepping out on me," she told him with a saucy, slow smile.

Jack paused as though he wasn't quite sure what to say and then shook his head again and held out his arm.

"It's time to dress for dinner," Jack said. "I'd love to try to persuade you not to nose into whatever that was, but I'm simply going to ask you to not get hurt again."

"Of course," Violet told him merrily. "I'll never get injured again."

He grunted as they walked into the house. "So you didn't grow up here?"

Violet shook her head. "We spent most of our time with Aunt Agatha and at school with just a little time with the rest of the family here and there. To be fair to my stepmother, we really were devils."

"Speak of the devil—" Violet caught sight of her stepmother, waggled her brows at Jack, and skipped up the stairs as though she didn't hear, "Violet? Violet! I'd like to speak with you."

She'd abandoned Jack and stopped when she hit the top landing. "Must bathe before dinner. Talk to you at dinner."

Jack shot Violet a look that promised revenge as Lady Eleanor cocked her head at him and said, "So you're the investigator."

Lady Eleanor was pretending she hadn't met Jack. She had, of course, when Jack had helped to solve the murder of her dastardly future-son-in-law. Fortunately for Isolde, her betrothed had been murdered before she'd been caught in his trap.

Violet's gaze landed on Jack. If he were her twin, Violet would have left him to it and done so with utter joy.

"Jack," Violet called, "St. Marks is calling for you. Also, Lady Eleanor, I saw Isolde looking for you in the kitchens. She's scared to follow through on St. Marks's offer. I told her to find you and get your opinion."

"St. Marks?" Lady Eleanor asked in a high-pitched squeak. "Offer?" The last word was a choked out spasm of joy and terror combined. "Afraid? What? Oh no—"

Lady Eleanor spun without another word and rushed towards the kitchens.

"That," Violet whispered, "was an example of true, true love. You should be honoured, sir."

"You threw your sister right under the carriage." Jack's face was blank, but the humour in his gaze told her how he truly felt.

"She'll be fine," Violet told Jack as he hurried up the stairs after her. "There are consequences to being the favoured child, and from me, it's a little light-hearted revenge. She's lucky that's all I do to her. It could be so much worse if I were more devilishly inclined."

Jack shook his head and pressed a kiss on Violet's forehead. "I suppose I should be grateful you use your powers for my benefit."

# CHAPTER SIX

Violet's bedroom had been decorated for her when she was in the schoolroom. She'd had no say in the purchases that had ended in layers of pink and maroon. She certainly hadn't chosen the canopied bed or the cushioned bench at the end of her bed. The only part she well and truly enjoyed was the pretty vanity with the hand-carved detailing.

Rouge yipped at Violet when she came into the room, and she rubbed the dog's belly, whispering compliments and love to her before she walked into the bathroom where Beatrice had been arranging Violet's things.

"My lady," Beatrice said with a smile.

Violet examined her maid, who was also one of Violet's favourite people. Her life was so much better with the maid in it. That being said, it was Vi's job to protect the girl.

"My stepmother invited Theodophilus Smythe-Hill."

The girl's gaze widened with concern and fear. It had been Beatrice who had saved Violet from the grasping hands of Theo. The poor girl had been a housemaid in Aunt Agatha's house when the fiend had decided to force Violet to accept his attention.

"Given our last interaction with Theo, I don't think he'll come."

Beatrice nodded silently, but the bobbing of her head was a little too quick, and informed Violet that the girl was not, in fact, feeling safe.

"I want you to stay with Lila's maid until we confirm that Theo isn't actually coming. I won't risk either of you, and I think we all know that the ladies won't be safe with that animal around."

Beatrice nodded, calming down.

"There is no order he can give you that you have to obey. You don't have to bring him tea, stoke his fire, or enter his room. There is nothing he can do to you. If he speaks to you, turn and leave."

Beatrice nodded again.

"If my stepmother finds out"—Violet closed her eyes, imagining how that would go—"she'll threaten you, but her threats have no weight. Remember that."

Beatrice took a fortifying breath. "Would you like a bath, my lady?"

Violet let the girl start the bath, adding bath salts and oils. Violet changed behind the screen and wrapped her kimono around her. She should hurry, she supposed. She hadn't checked the time, but she could tell it was pressing. She wasn't sure she cared.

She dropped into the bath while Beatrice offered dress options from the other room. "Choose whichever you like," Violet called. "Perhaps something scandalous as a special present for Lady Eleanor."

Violet lingered too long in the bath and then refused to rush through her makeup. Violet spun in front of the mirror. She'd been so focused on her thoughts that she hadn't paid attention to the dress until she examined herself in the mirror.

With a shimmy, Vi straightened the dress. It was a mix between bronze and copper with black lining and fringe. The beading was shiny and reflected the light. Violet's shoes were black with diamond buckles. Violet wrapped her favourite black pearls around her throat a few times. She added a diamond choker, diamond bangles, and diamond ear bobs. All the diamonds glittered along with dress, making Vi a shimmery beacon.

She winked at Beatrice through the mirror and then suggested, "Why don't you stay here in my room? Until Lila's maid can come join you."

"I hate being afraid." Beatrice glanced down at the carpet before lifting Rouge into her arms.

"You don't have to be afraid."

They both knew it wasn't true. Violet had been afraid a lot of times, and those experiences occurred when she should have felt safe. "What can I do?"

"I want to take Jiu Jitsu lessons as well." Beatrice pretty face was turned to the ground, her eyes fixed on the carpet. There had been a tremor in her voice, and Violet wished she'd have thought of it instead of making Beatrice ask.

"You should also choose other skills," Violet told the girl. "As much as I love you, I imagine the day might come when you'd be happier in another career."

"I love working for you." There was a plea in the girl's voice. It reminded Violet suddenly of the girl in the garden. Vi wasn't, however, the man in the garden.

"I could use a secretary or an assistant. I don't see why things should have to end with us, just...evolve."

Beatrice blinked and pressed her hand to her chest. "Really?"

Vi grinned. "Really."

There was a knock on Violet's door, and Beatrice opened it while Violet adjusted her bangles and touched up her lipstick.

"You're late," Victor said, leaning against the doorjamb. "The dinner gong rang."

"Yes, I thought I heard it," she replied.

"Denny, Lila, and Jack are in the hallway. Denny won't go down without you. He doesn't want to miss anything you do. Jack is getting antsy with you not appearing. He seems to think you will do something scandalous."

Violet grinned and crossed to him. She glanced down the hall.

"Are you trying to enrage dear Stepmother?" Victor demanded. "She's already furious."

It had been something of a personal revelation over the last few hours just exactly how angry Violet was. Her anger was nearly something she could touch. Violet tried to take in a deep breath and let the anger go, but it wasn't enough to reset her mood.

"She invited *Theodophilus Smythe-Hill* and some man meeting a girl in the gardens to this ambush of suitors. She invited money-grubbing fortune hunters to replace Jack. I'm *furious.* This smile is only because I refuse to wrinkle my face with frowns." Violet grinned merrily at the others.

"Uh-oh," Denny said gleefully. "Vi is on the rampage. A berserker with a pretty face. Will those nails scratch your stepmother to ribbons, darling?"

Violet took a long breath in, linked her arm through Jack's, and then put on that merry grin. "I suppose that Isolde, Tomas, and Gerald are in the family wing?"

"This isn't the family wing?" Lila demanded. "I was wondering where they were."

Victor shook his head, lifting Kate's fingers to his mouth for a gentle kiss. "The main family wing is the one that overlooks the gardens. You've noticed our rooms look down on the drive. We did receive rooms with balconies which were, of course, excellent for our mischievous adventures. A ready rope made of sheets, a tip toe down the drive, bicycles hidden in the bushes, and escape is at hand."

"But *your* rooms are here," Lila said slowly, her gaze darting between the twins.

"We were naughty children." Victor and Violet's gaze met and matching wicked, knowing, expressions crossed their faces.

"We were indeed." Violet trailed her finger over the hallway wall. "Those were the good days. I think we should channel them again. Did you see Geoffrey? Why is he the favoured child again? I feel certain that shouldn't be accurate."

Victor slowly grinned.

"I think we should start with the classics."

"Frame the boy?"

Violet's gaze glinted and her mouth twisted evilly. "We'll be at dinner—"

Victor lifted a brow. "How can we short sheet her bed if we're at dinner? Or put snakes in her bed?"

"Beatrice darling," Violet called, waiting until the maid joined them in the hall. "Would you and Lila's girl like to carry out some tasks for us during dinner? I'll give you both quite hefty bonuses."

"Why are we doing children's tricks?" Jack cleared his throat, but his eyes were twinkling. "Surely we're adults now."

"Because we can," Violet and Victor said in unison.

"Because it'll make her crazy," Violet added, since it was her fellow who asked.

"The little snake deserves it."

"Surely, we're better than this," Kate suggested. "He is your little brother."

"We *could* be," Victor said with a shrug.

"I want to see how far she pushes things while we uncover the nature of these lads," Violet told Jack, almost pleadingly.

"You want to delay telling her of our engagement?"

Violet nodded, searching his face. He wasn't pleased, but he only nodded.

They told the girls what to do, but it seemed Beatrice had a rather large amount of experience with pranks.

"We're going to talk about this later," Jack said, running his finger over her cheek.

"Violet? Victor? The dinner gong has rung." They turned towards their father and smiled as though they weren't conspiring. He examined both of them and lifted a brow. "Did anyone feel that? Ghost must've just crossed my grave."

Violet laughed and wound her hand through his arm. They had reached the parlor where everyone else had already gathered. Lady Eleanor made a comment, but Violet had already turned to the cocktail tray. Victor followed her to the bar cart and made them fresh drinks.

"There is a tray of drinks there," Lady Eleanor said sourly. "We've been waiting long enough for you."

"Apologies, sweet stepmother." Victor's grin didn't appease her. Though, of course, he hadn't stopped making drinks. She glanced at her guests and then waved her hand for him to proceed.

"This is deliciously awkward, isn't it?" Denny asked. Lady Eleanor sniffed and shot him a dirty look.

"Lord Devonsly made that tray there, Violet." Lady Eleanor nodded towards the tray and looked at Violet. "You should try one." It was an order, but Violet didn't move from her position next to Jack.

Standing next to each other, having come to the house together, surely Lady Eleanor knew that they were engaged or about to be? At the least? Yet...her gaze was moving from money-grubber to money-grubber.

"Oh, no offense taken," Lord Devonsly said, with a hound dog's grin. "I've heard Victor is a genius at cocktails."

"We've all heard that," Lady Eleanor countered. "That article—" She choked off her fury and tried for a genial smile.

Violet grinned, lifting the drink that Victor had made. He'd made cocktails, but he'd given her ginger wine. It was a good choice if he wanted to calm her down.

"You talking of that article? Heard about that at the club." Lord Devonsly shrugged. His eyes were cheery enough and his hound dog face flashed a self-deprecating grin. "I don't read much. Not a fan. I heard you are though, Lady Violet. You write books? That's what they were saying."

Violet grinned evilly as Lady Eleanor's jaw dropped. "Victor and I both do. We write together. My favourite"—her wicked smirk deepened—"is *Broken Surrender and the Scarlet Ghost.* We based that one off of Isolde. She was nearly manipulated into marrying a fiend just like our poor, heroine ingénue."

Lady Eleanor gasped, and Victor choked on his cocktail, staring at Violet as if he couldn't quite believe she'd say that.

"Not a fan of that one myself," Father said. "The poor girl's father was an idiot."

Violet winked at her father, who lifted his drink and saluted them.

"You read that trash?" Lady Eleanor demanded.

"Course I did. Other than the boys we lost, none of our children have done anything. Least these two wrote some books, had some adventures, tried their hand at *anything.*"

"Ah, yes," Isolde said. "That was a fun one. Tell me, Lord Devonsly, what do you do when it's raining if not read?"

"Oh, I don't mind the rain," he said sheepishly. "I'd rather be out in the rain than stuck indoors. I just put on the old Wellingtons, you know? Rain slicker. Have a big cuppa when I get back, all's well that ends well and whatnot."

"Did you quote Shakespeare?" Kate's head tilted. Her surprised glance moved to Victor and back to the others. The Nelson brothers laughed, though the young one seemed to enjoy it a little more.

"Didn't actually read it, you know?" Lord Devonsly chuckled. "I only remember the title. Those old boys at Oxford did just torment a fellow with expecting you to *read* things."

"Oh, I like him," Denny said to the room, then to Devonsly, "I like you. You're my second choice."

"Second choice?" Devonsly asked, glancing around. He blinked a little stupidly, and Violet shook her head.

Denny grinned at his wife.

Isolde cleared her throat, looking around a little frantically, and asked Lord Devonsly, "Don't you get ill?" To Denny, she whispered, "Stop it!"

"Hearty like a horse," Lord Devonsly replied.

Father stepped in, taking one of Victor's cocktails and then introducing the guests to one another. In addition to Lord Devonsly, there was the man Violet had met, Leopold Nelson, and his younger brother, Melrose Nelson. The fourth potential suitor was Kyle Rosens, who had traveled with his father, and far more interestingly, his sister, Celia. Could she have been the girl in the garden?

It must be Celia, of course it must. There were no other young women who could have been the one in the gardens. Violet watched the girl, trying to guess which of the four suitors might have feelings for her, but she seemed equally oblivious to them all. She was a good actress, better even than Violet. Unlike Celia's parent, Violet's father was watching her like a hawk—probably knowing something had spurred Vi's horse.

She considered getting well and truly zozzled just to infuriate her stepmother, but Violet didn't like to drink angry. Her gaze darted around the parlor, taking in the many men and few women at the gathering. It was heavily skewed towards gentlemen, something that would normally make Lady Eleanor furious. Instead, she'd done it to herself this time.

Violet glanced at her stepmother. The woman was so determined that Violet marry according to her desires that she was breaking her own rules.

"There's one more lad coming," Father added, drawing Violet's attention from her stepmother. "A Theodophilus Smythe-Hill. He was delayed but sent word he'd be arriving later this evening."

"Excuse me," Victor asked, "did you say Smythe-Hill?"

Victor, unlike Violet, kept his feelings on the subject in check. His voice was clear and even, his expression smooth.

"I did," Father replied. "Do you know the man?"

"We've—interacted." Victor's neck cracked as he struggled to hide the protective rage. "Did you say he's coming?"

Father nodded, and Victor's eyes narrowed dangerously. The usual lazy spaniel he wore as a mask faded, his lion coming out, and Father seemed to be well aware. Violet's head cocked as she examined Father. She'd always thought he was entirely out of touch with the twins, yet very little seemed to be slipping past him during this visit.

"Into a house with Kate, Violet, and Isolde," Victor muttered so low only Violet, Jack, and Father heard him.

"Is there a problem?" Father asked Victor, using a tone as low.

"There is indeed," Victor said. "Theodophilus will not be staying."

Victor was not asking, and he so rarely even shared an opinion that an order in Father's house was out and out shocking. Father blinked and glanced at Violet, who knew she had paled. No one had looked her way, and she'd been trying to gather her feelings in.

Father noted the change in Vi. "I see."

He might actually see, Violet thought, utterly surprised.

"Dear," Lady Eleanor said, stepping up to the small group, "let's not infuriate Cook by allowing her meal to go cold. I think we've lingered long enough for these two and their tardy friends."

Father grunted and took Lady Eleanor's arm, leading them into dinner. Lady Eleanor directed their seating, and Violet found herself between Lord Devonsly and Leopold Nelson while Jack had been seated in between Celia Rosens and Isolde. The table was quite unbalanced, but Violet could see that Lady Eleanor was pretending it didn't bother her.

Isolde had Tomas on her right. He had received a position of honour while Victor, Jack, Lila, and Denny were deliberately shuffled to the side. Jack was almost included, but Violet had no doubt his position was intended to keep 'Violet's suitors' away from Isolde and the triumph of her very rich conquest.

Denny seemed to prefer being shuffled. His eyes glinted with glee as he watched the players interact. He leaned back, sipping his wine, and Violet was sure his thoughts were something like, 'What perfect entertainment.'

Violet met her stepmother's gaze, glanced between her two table partners, and lifted a brow. Lady Eleanor smirked, and Violet's face hardened into sheer, cold fury. The look she got in reply was the sort of expression a parent might give an unmindful child. Violet let amusement fill her face and lifted her glass to her stepmother.

How Victorian could the woman be? Violet would no more allow herself or her fortune to be picked up by these fortune hunters than she would allow herself to be trapped into an engagement as Isolde had been.

"Do you really write books?" Lord Devonsly asked.

Violet turned to him. They had already discussed this once. "Is that so hard to believe?"

"Ah, a little?" He seemed uncertain of how to reply.

Leopold Nelson laughed low and mean next to Violet, but she didn't turn. Lord Devonsly might look like a hound dog, but he was a kind-hearted dunce. Violet wasn't sure she'd be able to use the word kind in association with the elder Nelson son after that laugh.

"You'll have to forgive Devonsly," Leopold Nelson said. "He seems to think his title will sell you on him."

Devonsly shifted next to Violet, and she noted the brilliant blush. Her gaze darted to Jack, who was leaning back watching avidly. She returned her gaze to Leopold. He wasn't handsome, but he wasn't ugly either. He had a sort of in-between unremarkable face until you noted his eyes, which were rather cold.

"And what do you have to offer?"

"Violet," Lady Eleanor hissed. "You must be exhausted after your drive to ask such a question."

"Oh," Violet asked lightly, "are we supposed to be play-acting at romance? Someone forgot to tell me that this wasn't just an auction."

Leopold laughed. "I, at least, have wit. Rather like you."

"Violet! Mr. Nelson! That will be enough."

Violet lifted her wine glass once more, saluting her stepmother and sipping the wine. Victor must have said something to the servant who had poured Violet her favourite calming drink. Vi closed her eyes, breathing in the scent and flashing back to Aunt Agatha. Many an evening had been spent with the two of them sharing ginger wine and talking. On one of those occasions, Aunt Agatha told her, "*Violet darling, you're the captain of your fate. Women have to fight harder, but sheer stubbornness will win the day for you, my love.*"

The memory of the woman who had actually raised Violet when Lady Eleanor hadn't wanted to try provided her with the surety that there was only one way this would turn out, and it would be as she wished. The rest was only drama for Denny to enjoy.

Violet didn't pay much attention to dinner, since her stomach, knotted with anger, made food rather unappealing. With Victor's commanding glances and Jack's worried ones, Violet ended up sipping a few spoonfuls of the soup and tearing off a few bites of bread, and then sipped her wine slowly, letting the soothing beverage comfort her.

# CHAPTER SEVEN

"Violet darling, give me your arm out of the dining room. We haven't gotten to say hello yet."

Violet slowly rose and joined her stepmother at the end of the table.

"What do you think you're doing?" Lady Eleanor hissed. "These are well-connected young men, and you are showing yourself to be entirely unappealing."

"I'm sure you've given them the family rumors of my inheritance to entice them here, Lady Eleanor. My looks, wit, and personality are rather of unaccountable value next to the carrot you are dangling before them."

"You will contain yourself and put on your manners or..."

Violet stopped, meeting her stepmother's gaze, and asked coolly, "What will you do?"

"Do you think your father will approve of your behavior?"

"I seriously doubt it," Violet told Lady Eleanor. "He appreciates the shield of manners."

"Therefore, you will—"

"He doesn't, however," Violet said, cutting off Lady Eleanor, "have anything to use as a control on me. My allowance, should he choose to revoke it, is certainly no longer needed."

"Would you say the same for Victor?"

Violet paused. "Are you saying that you will punish my brother if I don't choose from among your fortune-hunting—"

"It's an exchange, Violet. You bring the money, they bring the position, and you both benefit. This is the way of our people. For generations, we have done things this way. Supposedly you understand business. Set aside whatever romantic foolishness you wish to pursue and take advice from your elders."

"You engaged Isolde to a man as old as Father whose business was fraudulent. Please forgive me if I don't find your opinion on my future all that valuable."

Lady Eleanor gasped but then leaned in to hiss, "Then prepare Victor for a cut in income."

"What's all this now?" Victor's smooth, even tone made Lady Eleanor start.

Violet didn't bother to turn and face her brother. She'd guessed he'd followed from the beginning.

"Are you really trying to blackmail Violet into taking on one of your second-rate idiots by threatening my income from Father?"

"I—" Lady Eleanor's mouth gaped like a fish.

Victor's head tilted threateningly. He looked like a lion determining whether the mouse was worth the effort of catching. "Shall we call him over and ask him?"

Lady Eleanor started to speak. "How dare—" She faded out as Victor held up a hand and cut her off.

"We are not children anymore." Victor's voice was low, even, and commanding. "There is no scenario where you get your way when it comes to who Violet spends the rest of her life with. I suggest you look for an elegant way out of this mess you created and a way to apologize to her that won't ruin your relationship with her. We've forgiven you for a lot over the course of our lives," Victor said in that low-furious whisper. "I'm not sure that this will be one of those things."

"You've forgiven me?" Lady Eleanor gasped again. "You were horrible children."

"Of course we were." Violet glanced at Victor. "You didn't like us, and you didn't want us. Why would we behave?"

Violet placed her hand on Victor's arm, and they walked into the parlor as the younger Nelson brother, Melrose, said righteously, "I don't drink gin or cocktails. One glass of wine with dinner is sufficient for all."

Victor snorted. "You don't drink cocktails?"

"Alcohol turns mankind into animals." Melrose sniffed and then sipped from his tea. "Don't you agree, Lady Violet?"

Vi tilted her head as she examined the younger Nelson. "No. I believe that over-indulgence and lack of self-awareness turns mankind into animals. I also don't believe mankind needs alcohol whether it be gin, whisky, or wine to excuse their behavior. I've met far too many men who were animals without using a cocktail as the reason."

"Oh ho," Leopold Nelson said. "Looks like our Lady Violet enjoys cocktails, brother. You've just lowered your standing with her. Didn't you claim while we were out shooting that Violet would fall into your arms like all women do? What do you think, Celia? Have you also fallen into Melrose's arms? Shall we line you all up and see who succumbs first?"

Denny's delighted laugh prevented anyone else from having to reply.

Violet glanced at her brother with an order. He nodded and crossed to the cart where the bottles his man had added to the collection had been placed. Mr. Giles was always careful to pack Victor's own selections of alcohol and place them on whatever bar or bar cart was available. Nearby was the tea and coffee cart, and Victor busied himself at both.

Violet took a seat between Denny and Jack and glanced at Lila.

"Did you get told off?" Denny asked in his stage whisper. "I am so excited to be here. Violet, this place is better than Cuba."

Violet winked at Denny as Victor approached with a teacup. "Coffee, chocolate liqueur, blackberry liqueur and cream. I've been playing a little. It contains all of your favourite indulgences except ginger wine. Coffee, chocolate, and a cocktail. You're welcome."

Violet took the drink with a sigh and reminded herself that she didn't drink angry and she'd be sipping this magical creation slowly without refills.

"I'll have one of those, my lad," Lila said.

"Me too, please, Victor?" Kate glanced up at Victor through her lashes. She whispered to the others, "You know, your stepmother is significantly more challenging than my mother. I hadn't expected that."

"One can never expect Lady Eleanor," Denny told Kate, not bothering to lower his voice. He got a nasty glance from the lady in question but didn't even notice.

Victor grinned at his secret fiancé. "Darling one, I saved your cocktail for next so it would be the warmest. I know you like your drinks on the border of burning a hole in your mouth."

"That will keep me up all night," Denny declared. "I need something else."

"Something stiffer," Jack suggested, glancing at Violet. "Your demand of what the elder Nelson brother had to offer was everything I was hoping for, Violet."

Victor grinned and left, returning with three more drinks. While he'd been delayed, Denny had waxed near poetic until Lord Devonsly had appeared and taken a seat. He held a bourbon in his hand and grinned at the others affably.

"Not a cocktail man myself," Lord Devonsly said. "Or wine really. Drink it with dinner, of course, but I prefer a good pint or a bourbon."

Denny tilted his head, his eyes filling with glee. "What exactly did Lady Eleanor offer you as regards to Violet?"

Lord Devonsly shrugged. "Said Lady Vi would be coming around, had quite an income, and was looking to settle down. To be honest, she tried to—ah—allude to it, I think. Only I didn't quite get what she meant. Finally, your mother had to lay things right out for me. Couldn't imagine you wouldn't be able to find a fellow on your own. But maybe you want a title?" He sounded hopeful and turned those hound dog eyes on Violet.

She shook her head.

Denny cackled. "I can just imagine it. I see it in my mind. By Jove! To have been the fly on the wall for that conversation."

Lord Devonsly nodded. "Honestly, I would have thought I misunderstood if your mother hadn't had to lay it all out for me. Expect she's a bit confused about what you were wanting."

"That's one way of putting it," Violet muttered, as Victor handed Lila and Kate cups of coffee and returned with drinks for himself, Denny, and Jack, and then took a seat.

"What's all this now?" he asked.

"Your stepmother," Lila said, her gaze fixed on the girl, Celia, and the two Nelson brothers, "seems to have straight out offered a chance at Violet's fortune to Devonsly here."

Lord Devonsly flushed and glanced at Victor. "Thought it was worth the chance. Been a bit hard up lately. I figured even if things didn't work out with Lady Violet, there would be good shooting."

Victor shot a daggered glanced at his stepmother, who was studiously avoiding looking their way. She was chatting with Sir Rosens and his son, who had been the only one who hadn't bothered Violet yet. She supposed it was only a matter of time.

"I feel a little like a mare at market," Violet told the others, not caring that Lord Devonsly heard.

Lord Devonsly laughed. "You've got a way with words, Lady Violet. You should consider those Nelson fellows. They've got a way with words too. A bit sharp sometimes, but always so clever."

Violet saw Jack's jaw clenched, and Violet answered with the truth. She appreciated Jack's patience with her, and she suddenly realized that any revenge against her stepmother would never be more important than putting the man she loved first.

"I've already found a clever lad, Lord Devonsly. Have you met Jack Wakefield? I fear my stepmother has wasted your time. We've come to tell my family of our engagement, having no idea she'd engineered this party."

Lord Devonsly's mouth dropped. Jack's penetrating gaze met hers and she smiled gently at him. She should have realized that nothing else mattered—not even knowing how far her stepmother would carry this travesty.

"Stepmother, Father," Violet said, smiling up at Jack with actual worth before her expression cooled as it settled on Lady Eleanor. "Congratulate us. We've decided to be married."

Father immediately rose and crossed to them, shaking Jack's hand and kissing Violet on the cheek. "Been wondering. I gave Jack my blessing some time ago. Would have thought to hear by now."

"You did what?" Lady Eleanor demanded.

They ignored the question as Violet answered her father. "I was secreting my good luck away for myself. Savoring it, really. Aren't I the luckiest woman?"

"Good family, good head on his shoulders, good history. You could have done far worse, my love. Didn't expect to actually like my sons-in-law. Yet here we are. Your young friend, Tomas, for Isolde and one of the few fellows I'd trust with your wild ways for you. Couldn't be happier."

Violet laughed and kissed her father on his cheek in return. "Thank you, Father." Her whispered carried low and only to him.

His return whisper wasn't surprising. "Suspect your mother might have wished for a different timing."

"Father," Victor announced, cutting in. "No one will be surprised to hear that Violet and Isolde have fallen in love with clever, good men. On the other hand, prepare yourself for an astounding shock, sir."

Father's brow wrinkled, but his gaze settled on Kate, and a small smile twitched about his lips.

"Kate Lancaster," Victor smiled at her, "who speaks four languages, is learning Greek, loves literature, and reads scientific journals, has still somehow determined that I'm worthy of her hand."

"I appreciate," Father said, "how you listed out her brainy attributes. One might wonder if she were a bit slow if you hadn't."

Victor laughed and clapped Father on his shoulder while Lady Eleanor's jaw dropped. Her eyes were glinting with fury. They'd gathered the attention of the group and left her out of their announcements. It had been cold and deliberate and—in Violet's opinion—deserved.

The eyes of most of the group were on them, and Violet dared a glance around, noting a smile on Lord Devonsly and two matching scowls on the Nelson brothers, who were alternating between glaring at her to glaring at each other.

Violet accepted Lady Eleanor's kiss on her cheek, unsurprised that her stepmother's lips did not touch her cheek, hearing instead, "We will be talking of this."

Violet pulled back, winked, and linked her arm through Jack's. "Champagne cocktails, Victor. We're celebrating!"

Lady Eleanor's eyes widened as they turned her post-dinner matchmaking party into a cocktail party. Denny turned on the wireless with a sense of joy that seemed to rival Lady Eleanor's irritation. She looked as if she were about to say something, but Father leaned down and whispered to her.

Denny found jazz on the wireless and, with a wicked grin, invited Lila to dance. In moments, they were all dancing, Lord Devonsly joining in with Celia. Violet grinned at the other woman she'd barely talked to, noting how Celia seemed to be enjoying the evening far more now that she was no longer the unwanted single woman who didn't have a fortune to offer.

"Violet," Denny said as he, Lila, Jack and Violet caught their breath on the side of the room. "You are my favourite too. Sorry, my love."

The evening turned from awkward to downright hostile as Jack and Violet celebrated while everyone else seemed ready to string up Lady Eleanor. Violet felt about as sorry as she'd have been for the villain of one of her books. Speaking of—

"Victor darling," Violet said merrily, "I have the most delightful idea for our next book."

"Don't speak of it," Lady Eleanor said. "You must stop writing that...that...trash immediately."

"Oh sweet stepmother"—Victor's wicked grin wasn't able to pull out an ounce of sympathy from Violet—"we'll never stop."

"You have no need of the money," she snapped.

"You never know when one's allowance will be cut off." Victor glanced at Father, who simply lifted a brow.

"Have you done something worthy of having your allowance cut off, Victor?"

"One never knows." Violet wound her arm through Jack's. "I have been wanting to show you the folly here."

Jack's mouth twitched, and Lady Eleanor frowned. Father, however, only said, "Mind the walk, Vi. The path needs to be smoothed out."

Violet led Jack through the house and into the back garden. They were, she knew, being rude. She should have stayed and talked weather and been willing to dance with the other gents and let them try to romance her, but her anger with her stepmother didn't allow it.

She wound her arm around his elbow. "I shouldn't have delayed telling her. This is all my fault. I should have simply told her that we were engaged and let her rage."

Jack started to reply, but they both heard an auto on the drive. The gravel was spraying into the green, and Violet pushed up on her tiptoes to see who it was.

"It must be Smythe-Hill," Jack said.

She curled into his side. She was brave in the face of many things, but what had happened with Smythe-Hill grabbing her and manhandling her had burned its image into her brain.

Jack put his forefinger under her chin, turning her face up to his. "There is no way that he will hurt you again, Vi."

She nodded.

He smiled at her and pressed a kiss to her forehead. Violet laid her head against his chest. Jack was a large man, and when he pressed close to her, she felt as though she had a shield to protect her from whatever life may throw at her. Violet curled herself into him again. There was a time shortly coming when these wouldn't have to be stolen moments.

Violet let Jack hold her as they watched Theo Smythe-Hill get out of the auto with his man, who took his cases around the back of the house while Theo made his way up the steps. What would happen now? She wanted to be independent. She wanted to be strong and brave and ironically funny. There was at least a piece of her, however, that quaked a little to see a man walk into her home knowing he little valued what she wanted—even when it came to her life, her body, and her money.

## CHAPTER EIGHT

The folly at her father's house was, like so many, a Roman ruin. His looked like a temple that was somehow both still standing and on the edge of falling down. The looks were, however, deceiving. The ruin was a snug little building that kept out the elements when it was raining and was an excellent location to read a book on a lonely, grey day, assuming one also had a warm blanket.

Violet and Jack spent too long in those walls for even her father's sensibilities and when they came out, her hair was a bit mussed and her lipstick was gone. Violet grinned at Jack as they walked, fingers tangled, back to the house. They went through the kitchen door and found Cook still in the kitchen.

"Well now," Cook said, placing a plate on a tray.

Violet introduced Jack to Cook and winked when she got a knowing look from the woman. There was a sandwich on a plate with a pickle on the side, some sliced fruit, and a bowl of soup. Violet glanced the tray over and sighed for Cook, who had long since earned the right to return to bed.

"Is that for Smythe-Hill?" Jack asked, following Violet's gaze.

Cook nodded. It was necessary to know the woman rather well to see the level of her irritation as she made up the tray. It was well past the time when the kitchens should have been shut down and Cook able to relax however she preferred. Vi wouldn't have been surprised if it had been with pulp novels like Vi and Victor wrote.

Violet decided to snag a plate of biscuits since Cook was there to scold them over digging through the cabinets. Violet grinned at Cook, who seemed inclined towards being irritated when she'd normally make a plateful of biscuits for Vi and tell her she was too thin.

"I need to speak with your father," Jack told Vi. "He'll be in the library?"

Violet nodded as Cook called for the maid to take the tray up to Theodophilus. Violet examined the girl. "Call for a footman instead, Cook," she said. "Keep the girls away from him until Father and Victor send Theodophilus on his way." Violet said his name as though it were an insult.

Cook's eyes widened and then narrowed. She turned to the maid who had been waiting to take the tray up and said, "Go get Jordie."

Violet looked at her plate and thought what she needed was some ginger wine to go with the biscuits. If she were still able to curl into Aunt Agatha's lap, Violet would have taken her wine and biscuits up to her aunt and told her about Stepmother, the money-grubbing fortune hunters, and Theodophilus, who was so stupid as to believe he had a chance with her.

Perhaps instead, however, he thought he might be attempting to persuade Isolde. The fool! Lady Eleanor might be willing to throw Violet at anyone with the right connections, but Isolde was an entirely different story.

The parlor had emptied while Jack and Violet had escaped to the folly. The fire was out, the lights were dimmed, and the remnants of the mess—if there were any—were hidden by darkness. Violet left the lights down as she hurried towards the bar cart. The ginger wine bottle was familiar, and she would be able to find it in the dark.

She'd rather feel a half dozen bottles for the right shape than be forced to talk to someone other than her friends, Jack, or Victor. Violet was running her fingers over the bottles until she found the one with stars on the bottle. Just in case, she pulled out the stopper, sniffing it to ensure she'd had found the right bottle, and then she lifted her plate of biscuits again. Violet stepped towards the door on the opposite side of the room from her entrance and immediately tripped, crashing down and sending the plate of biscuits flying.

"Oh!" She pressed her hand down to push herself up, noting that the wine had spilled. Her hand was covered in liquid, and she could already hearing her stepmother's scold about the carpets. "Ouch," Vi muttered, taking a deep breath and pushing herself onto her hands and knees.

Vi paused as she wiped her hand on her dress. That was awfully warm wine.

A sense of horror hit her as she recognized that copper scent combined with the scent of gin. Gin—not ginger wine. Yes. That was a scent she knew and never wanted to smell again.

She took a breath and held it, filled with horror and the need to scrub her hands on her dress over and over again. Her skin crawled as she moved away from the...by Jove! Her breath left her in a rush. It must be. It must be. She pushed to her feet and hurried to the wall, finding the light switch. The moment the light was on, she took in a slow, horrified breath.

Too many bodies haunted her dreams. Too many unseeing eyes. But—oh goodness. She had to look, didn't she? Violet glanced down and saw the streak of blood on her dress. She slowly turned her hands over and found one smeared. She closed her eyes and hurried out of the room.

Coward? Perhaps. But she didn't need to have more fodder for those sleep-ruining dreams. Violet ran through the quiet halls towards the library where her father tended to read late and snooze by the fire until his man came for him and prompted him to bed.

Father and Jack were drinking by the fire, quietly talking when Violet burst into the room.

"Violet!" Father said, taking in the blood.

Jack said nothing as he crossed to her. He took her in and demanded. "Where is it?"

"The parlor."

"Who?"

"I didn't look. I tripped over it, in the dark, and I didn't want to add it to my..." She trailed off, but he seemed to understand. He'd learn with even greater detail when they were finally married and her dreams woke him up. Poor young Mr. Allen in the water. Poor strangled Harriet and always, always Aunt Agatha. The horrible Danvers. It was too much for one girl to carry around in her head. Vi didn't need to see their bodies for her mind to translate those who had been murdered to someone who had dead, staring eyes.

Violet knew that it didn't compare to what others had experienced. So many of the people in her life had been through the war personally rather than the comfort of home and schools, but even still—

Violet shrugged off her bad thoughts as Father and Jack hurried to the parlor, leaving her behind in the library. She glanced around at the floor-to-ceiling bookcases, the leather chairs, the crackling fire, and she shuddered. Tears were burning in her eyes, and she wanted Jack. He, however, couldn't take care of her and whomever was dead at the same time, so Victor would have to do.

Violet left the library and ran up the stairs to her bedroom. This floor and wing was only her friends and family. She banged on the first door and found Denny and Lila had that bedroom. It wasn't that she didn't know where Victor was—it was that she wasn't thinking at all.

Denny took her in. "Are we burying the body, darling, or has someone else committed the crime?"

Violet blinked stupidly. "Someone else."

"Ah, still in shock?" he asked. The humour fled as he started to connect that the blood on Violet's dress was someone's life blood. His voice shook a little as he asked, "Are they dead?"

Violet nodded. "I...I was looking for Victor." She just hadn't...it was just...oh goodness, she'd fallen over a body. Someone had died, and she'd tripped and landed in the blood. What if they hadn't died? What if whoever that was had needed help? What if she'd made it worse? Why had she run? She knew, of course, it was the dreams that had turned her into a coward.

"Let's get you to the bath," Lila said gently from behind Denny. "Darling, find Violet some ginger wine."

"No!" Vi shook her head frantically. "I tripped over the body. I spilled it everywhere. Oh, my goodness. The smell. Gin, blood, and ginger wine." Violet shivered and let Lila lead her away while Denny went for Victor. "Maybe—ah—dare I say just tea?"

Lila shuddered but called for tea. Violet moved without thought, allowing Lila to lead her to her room, draw a bath and wash her hands while it filled, and then help her settle into the hot water.

Violet could not stop reliving finding the body. She was babbling, she was sure, but she couldn't seem to stop.

Lila shoved Vi's head under the water. She came up sputtering and coughing. Beatrice had arrived with the tea and said, "Oh my lady. Are you all right?"

Violet was too busy coughing to answer. "She's fine." Lila unsympathetically handed Violet a cup of whisky and made her swallow it down quickly.

Vi gasped against the burn and then wiped the water out of her face.

"Are you done being feminine and weak?"

"No. Maybe. Stop it. I am feminine." Violet sniffed and shuddered into her bath and whisky. "It's awful, Lila. Do you know how often I dream of the dead bodies? Of the staring eyes? Of the murderer in the shadows?"

Lila took a seat on the edge of the bath and flicked some of the bubbles towards Violet. "I imagine quite often, darling. I suspect you'll have to firm up, however. You're marrying a man who's quite good at solving crimes. I don't suppose you'll avoid this—"

Kate opened the door to the bath, cutting off Lila, and took in the sight of Vi in the bath holding the teacup of whisky. She glanced back out of the door. "She seems okay, Victor. At least Lila is pouring a drink down her throat anyway. Maybe go and get her some ginger wine?"

"Not ginger wine," Vi said. "You can't go to the bar cart. It's... that's...I was getting some ginger wine in the dark, so I didn't end up trapped by any of the money-grubbers, and...I tripped."

Kate left the door cracked so Victor could talk to her and crossed to the sink. She handed Violet her cold cream and a washcloth before taking the tea and giving it to Lila. Kate pressed a gentle hand on the top of Violet's head. "Your mascara is running, darling."

"Vi," Victor said on the other side of the door, "are you saying that someone murdered a fellow by the bar? The bar? By Jove! Why there? Of all places? My heavens—"

Her voice choked in her throat for a moment as she felt the warmth of the blood on her hands again, remembering that moment of looking down at her dress and discovering it stained in red. That fresh horror of realizing she hadn't tripped over a misplaced pillow or wrinkle in the carpet, but she'd tripped over a body.

Lila watched Violet with a twisted mouth. "You were bloody, Vi. Drain the bath and scrub down again."

Violet shuddered and obeyed while Kate joined Victor in Vi's bedroom. They'd called Beatrice for more tea and Giles for some of Victor's private stash of alcohol, and Violet listened to her brother with his beloved while she scrubbed her body again. All signs of blood were gone, but the sheer idea of it made her skin crawl. She finished rescrubbing herself and simply dumped water over her body rather than sitting in the remnants again. When she was rinsed clean, Violet took the towel from Lila, who had gathered clothes for her.

Lila handed over undergarments and Violet slipped them on, topping with a nightgown and then a kimono that fell to her feet. She shivered as she stared at her friend.

"That was horrible." Violet pressed her lips together and met Lila's gaze in the mirror. "A part of me wishes I looked to see who it was. I can't let it go, not knowing who died. What if—I should have at least looked."

"At least it wasn't one of us," Lila said. "I suppose we all hope it was one of your disappointed fortune hunters. They weren't happy after you and Jack disappeared into the grounds. The Rosens brother, Kyle, and his sister had a hissed fight that sounded like snakes. They were interrupted only by the snide comments of both Nelson men to your stepmother as well as an argument between those siblings. I think even Victor was happy when Theodophilus arrived just to break up the scene."

"What did Victor say to Theo?" Violet asked as she was stepping back into her bedroom.

Her twin answered the question. "I told him we'd speak in the morning."

"It was clearly a threat," Kate interjected.

"And what did young Theo say?" Vi asked.

"He gritted his bruised jaw," Kate answered, "and then ignored Victor, making rather effusive comments about the generosity of your stepmother. It was nauseating. Theo complimented her on anything that could possibly be worked into a quick conversation. I think Theo was hoping that your stepmother would keep Victor from getting him tossed from the house."

Victor snorted.

"Vic." Violet scrubbed her hands over her face. "I have to know who it was."

He nodded and rose. Before he left her room, he filled several teacups with whisky and a splash of tea, handed them round the room, and pressed a kiss on both Kate and Lila's foreheads.

"This isn't fair," Denny said from the hall.

"Oh stop whining, laddie, and go get us some of your chocolate." Lila grinned at her husband. "Then make yourself useful for once and help Victor find out who died before Violet runs through the house in her kimono and sends her stepmother into a rage."

## CHAPTER NINE

"Can we do the thing?" Denny asked as he and Victor returned. "We need a chalkboard. Make the list of names and say why they were the killer. That's my favourite. Let's talk about why everyone here is the killer."

Lila rolled her eyes. "You just like gossiping about everyone's secrets."

"Too true, my love," Denny said merrily.

"It might help," Kate cut in reasonably, "if we knew who died. It's torturing Violet."

"It was the younger Nelson," Victor said. "I didn't care to catch his name. Melvin? Melbert?"

"Melrose." Kate shook her head, not believing Victor for a moment.

"We probably shouldn't make light." Violet shivered. Having a name to go with the blood that had been on her body wasn't making it easier. "I— Oh—what's happening?"

"Father called the local boys," Victor said. "They'll want to talk to you. It seems he was just killed, so..."

Violet blinked, nibbling on her bottom lip and pulling her kimono tighter as though it could somehow shield her. She took a blanket and wrapped it around her shoulders. She knew that she wasn't quite right since she'd found the body. Perhaps a doctor would say she was in shock. Did others become used to finding bodies? To seeing the crimes humans enacted on each other? Violet shuddered again at the idea and knew that she never wanted the time to come when she fell over a body and landed in blood and just shook off the effects.

"Vi's a suspect?" Lila's wry voice broke through Violet's haze. "I expect Jack won't let that stand for long."

"If his reply to the local constable had any effect, I'd guess that the boy is quavering in his boots. He might have stuck to his opinion—based on that article—if your father had let it go—" Denny grinned mischievously and then cackled, rubbing his hands together. "I do like your dear old dad, Vi. He scared that poor constable into wetting himself, I think."

"Darling, only you would be delighted by someone losing control of their bladder or the mere idea of such an event." Lila held out her hand until Denny frowned, removing a small box of chocolates from his inner coat pocket. "Of course you brought one of the small boxes."

"Violet will only eat half a chocolate," Denny muttered. "She'll eat half of it, stare off into the distance, and start weaving clues together like Watson."

"Holmes," Kate corrected. She glanced at Violet as Lila handed the box to Violet.

"Whoever," Denny finished.

Violet wanted to smile as she watched them banter. She felt like she was being haunted by Melrose Nelson. The image of him talking down to them all about the cocktails. The way his eyes had lit on her with avarice. The echo of tripping over his body with the feel of his blood on her. By Jove! Why the blood? Was she cursed? Violet wasn't sure she believed in such things, but she felt as though her life might be a reason to believe in the supernatural. What else could explain her bad luck?

"Our suspects—" Denny started.

"Let Vi catch her breath. She's still seeing whatever she saw." Lila's head tilted. "What *did* you see, Vi?"

Violet drew a shaking breath. "I didn't want to get caught by the fortune hunters. Jack had gone off to find Father and bond or—whatever you boys do when you get alone."

"He was throwing himself at your father's feet and letting himself be cross-examined. Fathers like to terrorize the beloveds of their daughters. That is one of life's many cruelties." Denny feigned a shiver. "I was too weak for such things and having just seen your father in action, Vi—Jack must actually love you and not your money."

Lila rolled her eyes at Denny again and smacked his arm. "Jack has money enough. His friends are simply quieter about it. We've gone blathering about Vi's money and now it's of epic amounts. Sonnet-worthy, even."

"It was always epic even before you started blathering about it." Victor lazily took a seat near the fire and pulled Kate onto the side of his chair. "It's why there were so many who might have killed dear Aggie over her hoard of the green."

"Hoard? My goodness, Victor." Violet scowled at him. "Terms like that are what make fools like Theodophilus believe that your fists are worth the risk of the inheritance. The gossip over it might as well be pirate gold." Violet took a bite of one of the chocolates and set it on her tea saucer. She watched Denny out of the corner of her eye and hid a smirk. Teasing him was making her feel better than anything else. Violet took a seat on the end of her bed, wishing Jack were there to answer all of her questions. "How did he die?"

Victor cleared his throat, examining her with a gaze that knew her too well. "He was stabbed."

"With?"

"The ice pick. I don't see why the killer had to involve the bar at all. They used that new gin I bought and drowned the body in it. What was the purpose of that?"

Violet took another sip of her tea to hide her reaction. "Why the gin? Just angry about the comment about cocktails?"

"It's a waste of good gin," Victor said. "I—suppose it makes me callous, but I am angry that someone used one of my favourite things to snuff out the fellow. I'm not sure, do I have a moment of silence every time I open a bottle of gin? Do I think about what you can do with an ice pick? I don't want to be entirely unfeeling, but I think I might be."

Violet moved from her spot on the bed to the other side of Victor's chair, perching on the armrest nearer the fire. "It's okay to still love making drinks for people, Victor. It's your way of showing you care."

He blinked stupidly up at her, and she patted the top of his head.

"Darling." Violet met Kate's gaze, who was laughing quietly at the dumbfounded expression on Victor's face. "You make drinks for the people you love; you put effort into finding what they like and learning ways to put the ingredients together to make them happy. It's why I got coffee and chocolate tonight. Don't be slow, dear one. If you were a nanny in the nursery, you'd be stuffing your little ones with sweets and jellies."

Victor nudged Violet, nearly pushing her off of her perch, but grabbed her arm before she could fall. "I suppose you are right. About the cocktails, of course, not being a nanny. I'd be hiding in the corner from the children, hoping they didn't track me down and torment me."

Kate grinned at Violet. "He means that he adores you."

"I suppose he's all right," Violet told Kate.

"That," Kate said, running her fingers through the hair at the base of Victor's neck, "means she loves you too."

"Even if you are the lesser twin," Denny finished. "We really would be better off staying somewhere else. We need a room for gathering to discover the killer. Take our notes. You know. All that fun stuff."

Lila laughed, taking one of her husband's beloved chocolates. "Do you think you'll be of help?"

"I'll be like the Greek chorus. I'll provide warning and atmosphere."

"Did he just make a literary reference?" Kate's lips twitched as she glanced at the others. Her gaze returned to Violet, and those pretty eyes widened with concern on Vi's face.

Violet supposed she must still be too pale and not quite back to herself given the way everyone was treating her with kid gloves, except for Denny.

"So what happened after you determined not to get caught by the money-grubbers?" Denny asked. "How did you go from deciding to be sneakily flitting around the drawing room for wine to finding a body?"

Violet started to answer and found that Jack and a uniformed constable were in the doorway. With them was a man in a brown suit and official looking demeanor. Violet wondered why she'd left her bedroom door open and why everyone felt free to approach her room like this. The way the brown suit was examining her, she felt certain that it wasn't only the constable who had heard of Violet and made suppositions about her character.

"A question for which I also need an answer," the man in the brown suit said. "I am Inspector Wright."

"Lady Violet Carlyle," Victor announced for Vi. She glanced down at herself. The kimono did cover her entirely and wasn't terribly inappropriate. "I am her twin, Victor Carlyle."

"Perhaps I might have a few minutes?"

"No," Victor and Jack both answered.

"Not alone," Victor finished. There was a bit of—not quite tension—between the two men. They were both inclined to be protective of Violet.

"Did you want your father?" Inspector Wright looked between the two men. Violet wasn't sure if he was choosing the earl over the dueling brother and lover because it seemed easier, but the earl would hardly be a better choice. The constable winced from behind the inspector. Ah, that must be the fellow who had made inferences about Violet's character and already been educated by her father. Violet shrugged, standing and crossing to the end of the bed where a pair of shoes were ready to slip onto her feet.

"I'll need a few moments to dress," Violet said as she glanced down at herself again. The inspector blushed, but really, he should have sent for Violet and not come for her himself. She guessed the reason he'd come was so that Jack couldn't coach her with answers.

Everything about this was quite irregular, and she wasn't going to apologize for making them wait. They filed out while Beatrice handed Violet a pleated navy skirt, a new pair of stockings, and a blouse with a large, loose jumper over the top. Nothing about her was fashionable, but she was somewhat cozy. What she wanted—Jack holding her tight

—wasn't something she could have at the moment. She could, however, have the comfort of her large, manly sweater.

She opened the door after brushing her hair and placing a turban over her damp hair. She joined Jack and Victor, who were waiting in the hallway when she left her bedroom. The inspector was just far enough away to make utterly clear that something he said had bothered the other two.

Violet glanced at her brother, and he lifted a brow. She smiled slightly, and he looked at Jack. Their silent conversation passed with the inspector watching, not understanding that Victor was making sure Violet didn't need him and then making sure that Jack would protect Violet as though Victor were there. Vi's expression told them both she'd be fine on her own, but they were welcome to come torment the inspector with her.

Vi walked towards the inspector, noting the wrinkles at the corners of his eyes. They seemed to be more from frowns than laughter, and Violet felt a flash of sympathy. But then those cold eyes focused on Violet, and she realized that he was suspicious of her. Did she look like she'd murdered the man? Why would he automatically think it was her who was the killer?

Violet followed the inspector down the stairs as he said, "Your father has made the blue parlor available to us. It's quite late, I know, but we do need to get started on fact-gathering."

"I don't mind answering your questions despite the hour," Violet said.

Jack was pacing alongside Violet, and when she glanced his way, she could see he was angry.

The inspector gestured to the room, and Violet smiled at him prettily without stepping into the small parlor. "We'll wait for my father."

"Ah." The inspector clearly objected but didn't say anything.

Violet wasn't surprised to see Smalley nearby despite the lateness of the hour.

"Smalley, would you mind terribly fetching the earl." Violet placed the smallest amount of emphasis on her father's title. She would not be convicted of a crime simply because she'd been the unlucky fool to stumble over his body.

Violet refused to enter the parlor and stood by simply waiting, an insipid smile on her face, while the inspector looked between her and Jack. She had little doubt that Jack would have to be told to go before he'd leave her to an inspector inclined against her.

"Have you lived in the village long?" Violet asked the inspector.

"All my life," he answered. "Except for the war of course."

"Of course." She wasn't merry about it, but it was the expected answer.

"Didn't see much of you about."

"We were very rarely here." Violet heard movement and turned to her father, who lifted his eyebrows as if to ask what this was all about. "Jack and Victor would prefer that I wasn't questioned alone."

Father laughed, choking on a snort. She guessed that he would add something about her not being helpless if he hadn't already scolded one of the local constables about Violet's character. Father gestured to Violet, who stepped into the room. When Jack followed, Father didn't object, and Violet saw the inspector frown.

Violet crossed her fingers in her lap and placed her most pleasant expression on her face.

# CHAPTER TEN

"I understand that you spent some time with Mr. Wakefield in the folly?" The way the question was phrased made it seem quite...salacious.

Violet's gaze narrowed on the inspector. She didn't think he even saw her reaction. "I did."

"You were there when Mr. Theodophilus Smythe-Hill arrived?"

"We had just left the drawing room and entered the garden when his auto arrived."

Violet didn't elaborate. She didn't care for the tone of this man, and she wasn't going to indulge him.

"And then?" His lips twitched a little bit.

"Then I walked with my betrothed through a few of my favourite parts of my father's garden, where we talked about our future, kissed, and returned to the house after a while."

"How long?"

Violet shrugged. "I wasn't keeping track."

"Ahh." Again with the salacious inference.

Violet glanced at her father, but he seemed to be snoozing. She smiled at him. The big...big...faker. She'd bet her fortune Father was taking in every word and gesture despite his eyes being seemingly closed.

"When we left the drawing room, I had little concern for the time nor do I have a curfew, Mr. Wright."

"Inspector." He frowned at her.

"Of course," Violet said, with enough attitude to make him wonder if she was mocking him. She was, in fact, so she credited him as being a better detective than she would have thought.

"Did you have further questions, Wright?" Jack's voice was smooth and cool.

The inspector scowled at Jack. It must be difficult to be in charge of a case where one of London's most respected detectives was looking on. Violet might have been sympathetic if he wasn't so determined to focus his ire on her.

"So you left your lover—where?"

"I was in the kitchens, speaking with Cook. Jack and I entered through the kitchen door, spoke with Cook for a few minutes, who was making a tray. I made myself a plate of biscuits. Jack left to speak with Father, who was in the library as he always is at that hour, and I stepped into the drawing room to gather up a bottle of ginger wine."

"The bar cart was across the room on the other side of the body. How did you trip over it?"

Violet shuddered at the memory. She had thought to be sneaky and turned out she had been stupid. If she had simply turned on the light, she could have screamed, gotten help, and had an alibi. If she hadn't wasted the time moving through the room in the dark, digging through the cart, feeling the bottles rather than using a light. Instead, she'd practically rolled over the body, contaminating it and herself.

"I had hoped to avoid other guests."

"It was dark." The inspector's voice showed doubt, and Violet didn't blame him for it. It would have even been silly if it hadn't ended with a body.

"I knew I could find the bottle in the dark."

The inspector looked dubious.

"Victor always buys the kind that has stars on the bottle. You can feel them even when it's dark."

"Do you drink a lot in the dark?"

"Only ginger wine," Violet told him rather too honestly. "It's my comfort drink. If only I found comfort in warmed milk."

"Yes. Well." He glanced at Father and Jack as though to ask if they could believe it. Since they knew Violet, she expected they believed it quite well. "So you rifled through the bar cart in the dark. You must realize that makes no sense."

"Of course it does. You just don't have all the pieces to form your picture."

"Form it for me then," the inspector snapped, seeming to lose patience.

Violet simply stared unblinking until the man back down and then said, "Father."

Without even opening his eyes, Father said, "Her stepmother invited a slew of suitable lads here with the hopes of persuading Violet to throw over Jack. Of course Vi was slipping through the house like a burglar. She was stealing away their hope of living off of her fortune."

Inspector Wright's eyes widened, and he turned to Jack, who sat stoically to the side as though he were entirely unbothered by the conversation. "I hadn't realized you had motive as well."

"I don't," Jack said smoothly. "What I have is the heart of a woman who is not easily persuaded."

"Her money must be of a great potential loss."

"I have little need of her money," Jack said smoothly.

"I am a bit too well aware of the income of an inspector."

Jack crossed his leg and folded his hands in his lap. He didn't seem to need a reason to defend himself, but Violet was far more inclined to defend him than herself.

"Jack's family is wealthy and he has no need of an income. He works because he's excellent at discovering killers. It was for that very reason we met."

"Yet," he said to Jack, "you didn't catch the killer in time to save her aunt and now your betrothed is quite wealthy. Do I have the order of those events correct?"

Violet wasn't able to speak. She was roaring inside, a shriek of fury.

Her nails dug into the palms of her hands, and she was shivering with the need to let loose her anger.

"It's interesting that you're focusing on that," Father said to Inspector Wright with a bit of mockery. "James Wakefield, Jack's father, is one of the cleverest, well-connected men in the country. Jack has an income that exceeds that of my heir and has little need to allow a murder to take place on the off-chance that he might persuade my head-strong daughter to yield her heart."

The inspector started to speak, but you don't cut off an earl, and Father's telling pause choked the inspector silent. "You'll find if you did some actual investigating that Jack is wealthy in his own right. Violet is wealthy in her own right. The murderer of Mrs. Agatha Davies confessed to her crime and is in a mental asylum. Inferring that they had something to do with that murder is a road you would be quite unwise to take."

Again Inspector Wright began to speak and Father cut in. "Melrose Nelson had as much chance at persuading my daughter to marry him—even without Jack's existence—as does a snail. He was a dull, prosing, punctilious man with too much affection for rank and for expecting certain behavior from women. You can be assured, if they had become further acquainted, Nelson would have lectured my daughter, she would have mocked him, and they'd have ended their association with a unified dislike. If you suppose that aspersions on their character and inferences about their motives will get these two to confess to a crime they didn't commit, you are very wrong. If you think any jury will accept such rough-shod work, let alone your own superiors, you are again quite wrong."

"Your daughter had the best chance to have murdered Melrose Nelson."

Father's head tilted and he waited.

"She could have killed him," Inspector Wright tried again.

"So could have I," Father said. "Most of this blasted party had gone to their rooms yet I was on the main floor. Perhaps it was me."

The inspector blinked, his mouth gaping. "I won't have a fake confession, if you please, my lord."

"And you won't get one. From myself or my daughter. Be clear, however, that I wasn't, in fact, with another person for most of the time around Nelson's death. You think that somehow my daughter met Nelson by chance in the drawing room, incapacitated him, stabbed him, and then ran for us? All without a motive or reason to want him die?"

"He might have attacked her."

"She is quite capable," Father said. "But he had six stone on her and if he attacked her, she would have cried for help, and Jack would have slaughtered him while I looked on with satisfaction."

The inspector stilled.

"We'd then get rid of the body on my acres upon acres of property. I doubt you'd ever have found it."

"I..."

"That's not what we did, though, is it?" Father asked merrily. "Instead we called for you because one of the grasping sponges masquerading as house guests murdered another. It's a real dilemma."

"I..."

Father ignored the inspector to move the interview along. "Violet, you tripped on the body after you found the wine?"

Violet nodded.

"Then?"

"It took me a moment to recognize the scent of blood." Violet reached out and took Jack's hand. Her fingers dug into his flesh as she remembered the feel of warmth and that distinct smell. The unwarranted warmth on her hands that ended with the most horrible of realizations. "I pushed myself up and turned on the light. I didn't look at the body. I didn't want it in my head."

"Of course," Father said.

Vi glanced at him, biting her lip. Her voice quavered and she wanted nothing more than to crawl in Jack's lap as though he would be able to shield her from the memories. She knew he couldn't protect her from what was in her head—but it felt as though it might be possible. Or maybe he'd be able to distract her from the memories until they lost their power. "I looked down. I saw the blood. I knew the smell. I...I ran for Jack and Father. I knew where they were. Then, I left the body to them. I didn't, I don't...want it in my head. I knew that Jack could carry that burden. That he'd take care of the poor victim."

"You didn't even look?"

"I have bad dreams," Violet told Inspector Wright, giving him the chance to see the weight of those dreams.

"You've been involved in more than one murder case?"

Violet let the tears well in her eyes. It was too fresh after the feel of blood on her hand, and perhaps, too soon after the rage she had been feeling earlier in the day, the reinforced knowledge that her mother had died, her aunt had died, and Violet would be marrying without either of them. There was a little girl inside of her who had never stopped hoping for a mother, and every time she and Lady Eleanor had one of their little spats, Violet was reminded—yet again—that she didn't have one.

None of that had anything to do with the murder, but all of those emotions were jumbled inside of her with the horror of murder and the anger that the man she loved more than anything wasn't good enough for her stepmother. Even while Violet was a suspect in this crime, she knew she'd be safe. The man she loved would ensure that she never, ever, suffered for a crime she didn't commit. She felt as though he wouldn't let her suffer for a crime she did commit.

"My aunt," Vi's voice cracked again, "was murdered for her money. It was never clear who her heir was, so one of those heirs decided to kill her to improve her circumstances."

"You were her heir?"

Violet glanced at Jack, the loss of Aunt Agatha haunting Violet, and a tear slipped out. She wanted her mother and her Aunt Agatha to celebrate her wedding with her. This feeling taking over her was the reason she'd kept her engagement hidden. Lady Eleanor would never fulfill the role of mother like Aunt Agatha would have, and when Violet's day arrived, she'd have to marry with the hole in her heart of her missing mother.

"Technically, we all were. I inherited the majority, but we all received enough to change our lives."

"Why you?"

"Aunt Agatha tried to teach us all how to care for her empire. I was the only one who learned."

Inspector Wright grunted. "Tell me about the other deaths."

"My sister Isolde was to be married to a Mr. Danvers. He pursued her because his son was obsessed with Isolde. Father and son hated each other. Danvers somehow convinced my stepmother that he was a man of fortune, and my stepmother convinced Isolde that he was a good choice. His son, however, killed him."

"He also confessed," Jack told the inspector mockingly.

"The rest?"

Violet shook her head, and Jack answered. "The next four cases all involved people who were in the periphery of our lives. I was called in on the cases because I was nearby when the murder occurred. Violet's whereabouts on each of those cases were carefully tracked and documented. There was never any suspicion that she was the killer, though her own cleverness assisted in the discovery and apprehension of those killers—sometimes leaving herself at great risk and causing her physical harm. She is quite lucky, in fact, that she wasn't another name on the list of victims."

"This is all documented?"

"Of course. Documented with notes, supporting testimony, and confessions."

Inspector Wright leaned back and smiled affably as if he hadn't been a horrendous rat. "I did have to make sure. The rumors about her —well, I'm sure you're aware."

No one agreed with him, and he flushed slightly before clearing his throat.

There was a knock on the door that cut off the awkwardness before it could descend into something else, and the Inspector excused himself, leaving them in the parlor alone.

"I wasn't aware you'd been quite so at risk, Violet."

She looked at her father and pressed her lips together. She had deliberately left the descriptions of her wounds quite vague in her letters. Father's expression said he just realized what she'd done. She winced at his expression.

Father adjusted in his chair, glanced at Jack, shook his head, and said, "I can see I'll need to be discussing this further with you, your brother, and Jack."

Violet grinned winningly, but it seemed Father saw far more than she realized. So she shrugged and said, "I'm fine now, Father."

"Mmm." His simple reply didn't make Violet feel any better.

The inspector came back into the room. "There's sign that the gin was poisoned."

"Where did the blood come from?" Violet's question burst from her. He couldn't have been poisoned. He was very clearly injured in a way that left quite a puddle of blood. She gripped Jack's hand even tighter.

"He *was* stabbed," Jack told Violet.

Yes, she remembered, the ice pick. Oh heavens. Her stomach roiled with the thought. She wasn't sure knowing how he'd died and the instrument of his death instead of seeing the body was better. It seemed that the questions were nearly as bad as the images. She hated that she could compare the experiences.

"*And* poisoned?" Violet asked the inspector.

"According to the doctor, the bottle of gin was poisoned."

"Why?" Violet shuddered. "Were there two would-be killers or one person who wanted to be very, very sure?"

Jack shook his head, but no one had an answer.

# CHAPTER ELEVEN

When Violet returned to her room, she wasn't surprised to find the chalkboard despite the late hour. She was, however, surprised to find Kate sleeping on the end of her bed with Victor sitting next to her, holding her hand. Then there was Denny writing neatly on the board—who would have even thought the lazy man had such perfect penmanship? That required actual practice, something Violet wouldn't have expected in Denny of all people. Lila was sitting near the fire, cocktail in hand, box of chocolates on her lap, feet up on the opposite chair.

"This is all quite unexpected," Violet told them. She read the board over. There were neat lines separating the names of everyone in the house. Denny had included young Geoffrey but left off the servants.

"Just starting the best part," Denny said, glancing over his shoulder with a grin.

"I was a suspect," Violet told them all at once. "They asked very insinuating questions of me. Miss Emily Allen struck harder than she knew with that article of hers. Between Father and Jack, I believe I've moved down the suspect list, though I am certainly still a person of interest."

"Where is Jack?" Victor asked with lifted brows and a frown that said he was displeased Violet had returned alone.

"Speaking to the doctor about a rather startling revelation."

Denny held his hands out for the information as if receiving a rather exciting gift.

"It's a bit morbid, my lad, how much you enjoy this madness."

He grinned unrepentantly and without an ounce of shame. "Darling Vi. I didn't do the killing. I won't apologize for admiring the way your mind works."

"Jack is a much better investigator than I am," she told Denny. "Why aren't you following him around?"

"Yes, darling, we all know that. The problem is Jack! He follows the rules and walks the straight path. He won't give details. You, my dear sweet devil, you follow the rumors, pry into the secrets, put them all up neatly on the board, and string them together as though you're making a necklace."

Violet paused, stepping back. "Victor, wake up your love and take her to her bedroom."

"I'll make sure she's locked in and then come check on you, darling Vi." Victor didn't wake Kate, just lifted her into his arms. It was odd, Violet thought, that Kate was tired. Was she getting sick? If she did, would they get sick too? Violet couldn't imagine anything worse than being truly ill in Lady Eleanor's home. It was bad enough being ill when Victor turned into a mean infant.

Vi glanced at Kate and Victor and hoped it was only exhaustion. It had been a long night, and Violet was sure that if she wasn't feeling quite so haunted, she'd be craving her bed too.

"Out," she told Denny, glancing at Lila, who slowly put down her cocktail and cocked her head at Violet.

"Did you want me to stay with you? Denny can warm his toes on a hot water bottle instead of my feet if you need."

Violet started to shake her head no, changed her mind, and nodded. Denny crossed to Violet and kissed her on the forehead. "Don't carry this on you, little love. None of this is your fault."

"I can remember the feel of the body. The warmth of his blood. It hadn't cooled yet." She clenched her teeth, trying to find her bravery.

Denny nodded. His voice was gentle when he spoke. "There's no need to fear with Lila near. She's a dangerous creature, you know."

Violet laughed a watery noise.

"I expect that you were too tense when you got here, love," Denny told her. "Then with the nonsense with your stepmother—anyone would have a rough day after that. Only then to meet the sponges. Those men expect to pick you up like their own personal bouillon chest."

Violet blinked as Denny laid out all the reasons why she was in chaos inside of her mind.

"I mean, Vi." He seemed almost sympathetic. "I adore Isolde as much as any married man who isn't her sibling."

Violet laughed at that, but her laugh was too weak to really sound amused.

"She's sweet. Sweeter than you. Kind too. Looks up at a guy and is needy. The boys enjoy being needed. You're a bit too headstrong for most. Can't imagine it feels good to see your stepmother coo over Isolde and ignore you."

Violet paused. "It doesn't," she admitted quietly. Lila reached out, taking Violet's hand.

"Your stepmother rejecting Jack is painful. You knew she would, of course; that was why you kept your engagement quiet."

"Are you always full of insight and thoughtfulness?"

"I'm not an idiot." Denny grinned over his shoulder at his wife. "I'm lazy, my love. It's entirely different."

"To make matters worse," Violet said to them both, pushing Lila's feet down and taking the other chair. "We've added in a dead body, a bath in blood."

Even Denny shuddered at that idea. "That's a lot even for a callous soul like mine."

Lila sipped her cocktail and glanced at Denny. "You're not a callous soul, darling. You're a lazy soul."

"I can still shudder over that day. I'd have been whimpering in a ball on the floor after Violet's day. Look at her. She's only a little down."

Violet stared at Denny as Lila laughed. "You didn't think I fell in love with him because of his chubby face? He didn't even have money when we married."

"You fell in love with his secret thoughtful side?"

"He wrote me love letters," Lila told Violet, patting her heart and then winking at her husband.

Violet grinned suddenly, remembering the look on Lila's face each time one arrived. They'd exchanged them all through their school years even when they were in the same town. The memory of it was enough to push away the remaining horror.

"Who wouldn't fall in love with love letters?" Violet asked, sniffing. She took in a deep breath and let it out slowly. Once, twice, three times. "You don't really have to stay."

"You," Denny told Violet. "You fell in love because someone finally appreciated your cleverness. Everyone else saw your pretty face and your daddy the earl. All Jack needed to do was note that you were smarter than the average lass."

Violet laughed again before staring at the board. She crossed to the first name.

MELROSE NELSON—VICTIM.

Both stabbed and poisoned. Was he hated so much that someone needed to be absolutely certain he was dead? Or, perhaps worse, was he a victim twice over?

Lila took in a deep, horrified breath and wrapped an arm around Violet's waist. "What a terrible crime."

Violet nodded, staring at the board of names. At the end of the board where no names were listed, she wrote: Who was meeting in the garden, clandestinely? Her gaze flicked over the board and then she wrote: Why was the gin poisoned? Was there a second intended victim? Didn't Melrose only drink wine?

Violet bit her lip and wrote after Geoffrey's name: He was playing billiards with the victim. Happenstance or something else?

Violet tucked her hair behind her ear and played with the ring on her finger as she stared at the chalkboard.

The door to her bedroom opened, and Violet looked up to see Jack there, watching her stare at the board. His jaw tightened and that familiar look of worry appeared in his gaze. "Whoever killed Melrose is certainly in this house, Vi."

She nodded, crossing to him and wrapping her arms around his waist. She had been waiting for a hug from him since she'd found the body. "So you want me to stay with you or Victor?"

"I'll stay with you," Lila inserted. "I am, as my husband so beautifully described, a dangerous creature."

Jack laughed and pulled Violet closer. They weren't a couple for affection in front of others—not more than a kiss on the fingertips, forehead, or possibly wrist. Only having landed on a body, she needed a little more comfort than a kiss on the forehead.

"They are less inclined to believe it was you," Jack said. "The assumption was that you stumbled across Melrose and he attacked you. But then where did the poison come from?"

Violet pressed her face into his chest. Where *had* the poison come from?

"Seems like a bit of overkill," Denny told Jack, as he added a border around the chalkboard. "Both poisoning a fellow and stabbing them. Perhaps we should be looking for the person who was the most excessive."

Violet breathed slowly in. She had needed to feel Jack holding her. Was she a cipher now? This weak-willed wallflower who couldn't function on her own? Her mind immediately rejected the sheer idea. Violet would have carried on without Jack. She would have gotten through the evening and into the next day. She'd have faced the murder investigation as a more serious suspect without him, and she'd still have been all right. With Jack, however, she didn't have to do those things alone.

Being in love with him didn't weaken her. Not in the least, but being in love with him gave her a...what was the right term? A help. A support. A partner. All of those things wrapped in one over-sized package.

"Why would someone both get stabbed and poisoned?" Lila asked. She might have sounded more bothered if it were drizzling and her coiffure were at risk.

Violet shook her head against Jack's chest. She was just going to linger in this warmth.

"That," Jack said as he rubbed his hand down her back as though she were an infant who needed to be soothed, "is a problem for tomorrow, don't you think?"

Violet turned in his arms to face her friends. "I think we need to talk to these people."

The list read:

MELROSE NELSON —VICTIM

LEOPOLD NELSON —BROTHER

LORD DEVONSLY

SIR ROSENS (FATHER)

KYLE ROSENS (BROTHER)

CELIA ROSENS

Denny hadn't bothered to add any of the names of Violet or her family outside of young Geoffrey. What had he done to irritate the lazy Denny? She, however, added all the names of her family, including her siblings Isolde, Gerald, and her long-time friend Tomas. She didn't believe for a second that any of them had killed Melrose Nelson, but she thought they needed to know where they were and what they were doing at the time of the crime. Her stepmother, Lady Eleanor, Violet wrote with a flourish and added the shape of a small heart after her name.

Denny chuckled while Lila gathered up the teacups and placed them on the tray. While Violet was gone, Beatrice had straightened the room, leaving only Vi's nightgown and kimono on the bed. The maid had also taken away sweet Rouge. After her day, Violet would have welcomed a furry little dog to sleep with her. Rouge was about as fierce as a bunny rabbit, but at least her tail would flop and wake Violet if someone entered her room.

"Do you think Tomas or Isolde were involved with the murder?" Denny seemed to like the idea.

"No." Violet placed the chalk down. "I'm going to have to start traveling with one of these if we keep being so unlucky."

"I like the chalkboard version better than your journal," Denny announced. "Perhaps I will purchase one for you for your birthday. Some sort of transportable chalkboard."

Violet crossed to the board and wrote under Celia's name: Who was she meeting in the gardens?

"What's this?" Denny demanded. "In the gardens? A scandalous meeting? How did you not share this delightful news already?"

"Violet learned from the cook," Jack said. "The servants know everything. A fact that has helped me on more than one investigation."

"One of your money-grubbing lads was meeting another girl in the gardens and was also here for your money?" Lila arched her brow. "Is this Celia without pride? Is the fortune hunter a complete idiot? Surely they didn't expect to cheat on you in your own house?"

"I believe Celia seemed—" Vi glanced at Jack. How would she convey the tone? She was about done, Violet thought. Done with the lies. "She was calling him on his machinations. I would assume that she realized he had been manipulating her—whoever it was who was manipulating her. He seemed to believe he could tell her she was wrong and she'd accept it."

"Lads these days," Lila muttered. "They always seem to think women are as dumb as they are. I would wager our mothers and grandmothers were well aware of the character of the gents in their lives. They were just trapped in their marriages. The problem for modern lads is we're not so trapped anymore."

"If it was young Melrose, maybe the reason he died was the games he was playing with Celia. She has a father and a brother here. Depending on how—ah—far the lad took his manipulations, perhaps there was something worthy of vengeance from the father or the brother."

Denny shook his head. He really was too happy for a discussion about murder. "Victor would probably commit murder for you, Vi. I don't know if he would for Isolde. What brother would truly kill for his sister? My vote is for the father."

"We don't know it was Melrose in the garden with Celia. I think, however, that Victor is far more protective of Isolde than you realize," Violet countered.

"So he'd commit murder for her?" Denny's lips were twitching, and Violet scowled at him.

"Go away," she told him. "Leave your dangerous creature and get out of my room. When my head stops hurting and I stop reliving stumbling over Melrose's body, I will educate you in manners."

Denny was laughing as he left Violet's room, but it was edging towards well past midnight, and they had traveled that day. She'd have been exhausted even before the emotional runaway carriage ride she'd been on since arriving at her father's house.

Jack pressed a kiss on her forehead. "Don't worry about finding the murder victim, Vi. I'll make certain Inspector Wright does his job correctly. Don't worry, my darling."

Violet nuzzled her face into his chest. "Whyever would I worry when I have you?"

Another kiss on her forehead was her only answer.

## CHAPTER TWELVE

"You kick," Violet said into her pillow without turning her head to face Lila. Dangerous creature was right—the woman's feet and legs were a punishment when a girl was trying to sleep. "Go back to your spouse and leave my poor legs alone."

Violet could tell by her exhaustion that it was still quite early. She pushed her face mask back and saw Lila grinning her way. Light was starting to creep through the curtains in front of the French doors, but it was dim enough that Violet was certain it was still quite early. Lila was on the other side of the bed, but the wild woman slept at an angle. Violet vaguely remembered Lila patting Vi's back when she woke up to bad dreams, but she remembered far more clearly the feel of Lila's lashing feet.

"It's cold," Lila told Violet. "I don't want to get up yet."

"It's early too," Vi added, flopping back onto her pillows. Her gaze flit around the bedroom, landing on the door to the balcony, the chalkboard with the names, the closed armoire with Violet's perfectly placed dresses. She curled onto her side, glancing at Lila, and said, "No more kicking and I won't throw you out."

Lila grinned. "Denny wraps his arms and leg around me and holds me down."

"Sounds suffocating."

"His legs were covered in bruises for a while before he decided upon the smothering me route," Lila laughed. She pressed her face into the pillow and then a rare serious expression crossed her face. "Do you sleep like this often? You cry in your sleep."

Violet pressed her lips together. "Too often. It's been happening since Jeremiah Allen. For a while there, I couldn't close my eyes without picturing him in the water. He was so young; he looked up to Jack so. My dreams have changed, so it isn't Jeremiah looking up to Jack, it's our own son. Who then dies."

"My beloved friend," Lila said with a wince. She reached out and took Violet's hand. "That's horrible. Invite Jack to your bed, marry him if you don't want to invite him before the big day, sleep with a light on, use some of that lavender bath oil and take a bath before you go to bed every night, but you must do something. You have dark circles under your eyes. You didn't recover from finding that body as you have in the past. You're—"

Violet closed her eyes. She was so tired.

"You were crying in your sleep," Lila told Violet. "I was...well...you know I prefer to detach from most things, but I think you need help. I don't know what you need. Vi—it's like you're experiencing a lesser case of shell shock. What worked for Tomas? Maybe you need to go for walks like he did and focus on the good things and...write it all out?"

Violet didn't disagree. She might have fallen in love since she'd first met Jack Wakefield, but she'd also lost her near-mother, seen too many bodies, and been physically attacked. The time since meeting him to the current day had been difficult to say the least. Violet knew when the dreams didn't stop, she needed to do something. She just had no idea of what to do. And here she was again, facing another murder investigation.

Violet closed her eyes. She wanted to go back to sleep, but the dreams were hovering. Instead she made her way to her bath. Hearing Lila's counsel replay through her mind, Violet filled the bath with lavender oil and salts. She slowly sank into the water and reached towards her toes. She stretched until the knots from restless sleep faded in the heat of the water. Slowly, she scrubbed her body, trying to focus on all the things that were good in her life.

Jack. Isolde's return. The light in Isolde's gaze. Tomas finding happiness. The love in Victor's eyes when he looked at Kate. How very much Violet liked Kate. Vi had long carried the secret worry that Victor would eventually fall for a woman that Violet couldn't abide. She should have known better. She thought about the way the wind fell on her face when she and Jack walked in the gardens. The taste of chocolate melting in her mouth. The bitter, dark flavour of Turkish coffee. The way Beatrice's gaze had lit up when Violet had offered to train her to be an assistant instead of a maid.

Always and forever—Jack. Violet thought about the way his hand pressed against her spine when they walked. The way his eyes glinted when she teased him. The way he wound their fingers together. The friendship between Jack and Victor, and the way the two of them consciously determined to become brothers.

Even with all of those good things, she couldn't quite shake the darker memories. She lowered into the water until everything but her nose was covered, letting the water fill her ears and muffle the world. She had always loved the way everything became more distant when she buried herself in water. Violet took in a long breath and held it, trying to find some peace. Her mind jumped from her dreams to Jack, to Lila and her kicking, to the murder investigation.

The police wouldn't let Violet or anyone else leave her father's house until the murder investigation was over. She was guessing that she wouldn't sleep peacefully again until she was home and away from the murder site. Maybe not until she started sleeping with Jack's massive warmth as well. The idea made her shiver. She had never...they had never...it both sounded lovely and different, and—it was an odd thing really. She couldn't quite wrap her mind around a physical relationship.

She knew that Lila and Denny hadn't waited until they were married to be together. Violet hadn't ever allowed any previous relationship to reach that point. It was something she wanted with Jack, but—it was also foreign. Was that the right word?

Her mouth twisted, and she deliberately returned her mind to the investigation. The constable and the inspector had both jumped to Violet as the murderer. Or at least as the main suspect.

She slowly sat up in the water. What if that was just this inspector's way? What if he deliberately focused on each suspect, making them feel as though the only possible killer was the person in front of him? Maybe he hoped to scare them into revealing their secrets? She didn't think it was the best way to investigate, but the village was a quiet place and perhaps Inspector Wright didn't have experience with an investigation of this kind.

Vi wasn't sure it mattered what his theory about her was. She had to assume she was the main suspect and work to ensure her freedom. It was time to figure out who killed Melrose Nelson and all the other horrible things that were uncovered when someone was murdered.

Violet cracked her neck and pushed herself out of the water. Wrapping a robe around herself, she crossed to her bedroom. Lila had left while Violet was bathing, so she dressed quickly. She chose a long, brown, pleated skirt and an over-sized jumper over a high-collared blouse. Her selections were about as anti-bright young thing as she had, and she chose them specifically to play mind games with Inspector Wright.

She looked out the window and paused. There was a woman walking towards the back garden. Violet instantly wondered if that was Celia. The form was distant enough that Violet couldn't quite make out much more than the skirt. If it was Celia, Violet would be tracking that young woman down and asking her about the lover in the garden. It was time to start getting some answers.

Violet hurried down the hall towards the stairs but stopped when she heard someone yelling in the great hall. She stepped closer to the wall and edged forward to listen.

"What do you mean we can't leave?" Lord Devonsly said. He wasn't the one yelling. He sounded as affable as ever. "I just want to go shooting."

"We'd prefer for the weapons to be put up." Inspector Wright's firm voice carried up the stairs to Violet as if on fairy's wings. She grinned at the idea of a mischievous fairy carrying tales and tilted her head towards the gentlemen.

"What? Why?"

"Someone was killed here," Inspector Wright replied with baffled irritation. From the sound of it, he'd explained at least a half dozen times.

"But *I* didn't kill him," Lord Devonsly replied with the same blunt opposition. "Are you sure that there isn't a tramp? Can't imagine any of the folks here killing someone. These are good people."

"So you know them well?" Inspector Wright asked.

"As well as you know anyone. I quite like the Carlyles. Backbone of the country folk. Lost two sons in the war. Didn't try to sidestep sending them off."

"I'm sure you can understand"—Inspector Wright's voice was fully exasperated—"that we can't use the fact that they sent sons off to war as a reason to allow someone to get away with murder."

Violet peeked around the corner and watched as Lord Devonsly shook his head. To his mind, it was clear that Inspector Wright was the one who didn't understand. "That's what I'm saying. They *wouldn't* have murdered anyone. People like the Carlyles don't *need* to murder."

"What is that supposed to mean?" Inspector Wright demanded, shoving his hand through his hair. "Anyone is capable of murder in the right circumstances."

"But they can just ruin you," Lord Devonsly replied. "They don't need to *kill* a fellow."

Inspector Wright laughed, and Lord Devonsly groaned in frustration. Violet had to bite her bottom lip to avoid laughing aloud. Certainly Lord Devonsly was a bit of a blockhead, but he was also entirely correct. Violet's father had connections to the most powerful people in the country. He wouldn't need to commit murder to destroy someone's life. Why bother with murder when you can slowly torture someone until they give up on their own.

Violet would say her father would never do such a thing, but the truth was, if it were someone he'd consider murdering, he probably would do just that. Violet stepped back from the stairs. If she kept eavesdropping on the conversation that would never end in understanding, she might miss Celia.

Violet stepped backwards until she was out of sight and then turned and hurried towards the servant's stairs. She rushed down the darker, narrower staircase and appeared at the back of the house near the kitchens. Violet went quickly through the kitchen, winking at Cook as she went out the doors. The constable was in the kitchens, but Violet didn't let him catch her.

"You can't leave," he called.

"Just going into the gardens for some air," Violet replied without stopping. He'd have to follow her, or he would have to accept that she wasn't actually leaving.

She paused outside when certain he wasn't coming after her, glanced around, and rushed towards the last place she'd seen the young woman. She hoped that it was actually Celia and not some maid on her afternoon off. It took Violet a moment to catch movement in the gardens. She walked swiftly down the path towards the movement and stopped when she saw Celia leaning against a tree. There was a man standing in front of her, leaning with his hand on the trunk near her head so that he loomed over her.

Vi wasn't sure if she was seeing a man intimidating Celia or romancing her, and Vi wasn't sure who was in front of Celia. Violet had been loomed over by both Jack, and loved it, and Theodophilus, and hated it. She stepped forward slowly, an ear towards the couple.

"...see how you can just..." Celia said. Her voice trailed off, stealing the words from Vi. The tone, however, wasn't distressed.

Violet paused. If Celia wasn't being hurt and the couple hadn't heard Vi's approach—well, it was a good opportunity to learn some things, wasn't it?

"I'm broken inside, Celia! I—I—it's not easy. I lost my brother."

Violet took a deep breath. Was this Leopold? Violet re-examined the man. Of course it was. She really was out of sorts if she hadn't realized who the man was. Who else could it be? The Rosens man was as blonde as Isolde. Violet sighed at the way her head was chugging along so slowly and told herself to sharpen up.

"You did lose Melrose!" Celia said. "*Just* last night. And yet you're out here and you're...you're...my goodness, Leopold, mourn your brother and leave me be!" She glanced away from Leopold and found

Violet. Celia's jaw dropped, and she cleared her throat, shoving at Leopold until he too turned.

"What's this?" His tone was certainly threatening now, but what could he do? Any danger she faced from Leopold Nelson was a problem for later. Whoever the killer was couldn't be dumb enough to hurt Violet in front of witnesses. Really, the murderer was too clever by half. Both poison and stabbing? An eminently clever way to muddy the waters.

Violet met Leopold's gaze.

"What are you doing out here?" He was furious, his gaze lighting on Violet as though she were an interloper.

"Walking in my childhood garden," she lied. "Trying to clear my mind."

"Did you kill my brother?" he demanded. "How could you?"

"Why would *I* kill your brother?" Violet arched a brow at him. "You do realize that I have no reason to kill your brother. Unless you also believe that your brother attacked me in the drawing room and I was forced to defend myself? Somehow overpowering a man twice my size?"

Leopold scowled at Violet's mocking voice.

"It doesn't really add up, does it? You know what does add up? Siblings kill each other far more often than random strangers, did you know?" Violet smirked at him. "Often over jealousy of the same woman. Tell me, Celia," Violet said, looking over Leopold's shoulder, "was it Leopold or Melrose whom you've been walking with in the gardens?"

Leopold stepped into Violet's space, attempting to loom, and she felt a flash of fear.

"You'll need to be stepping away from my fiancé," Jack said.

She winced. That was the voice of exasperation. She stepped toward Jack without turning around. "What do you think, Jack? Has Celia been walking with Melrose or Leopold?"

Jack placed his hand on her back, and she felt instantly safer. "I think that you shouldn't be out here while there is a killer in our midst."

"Whoever did the killing isn't going to strike me down in the gardens."

"What are you trying to say, Wakefield?" Leopold demanded, his gaze going between Violet and Jack as though he couldn't believe what they were insinuating.

Jack's fingers dug into her spine, and she was sure that he wanted to shake her. "Violet, my love, Melrose was murdered in the *drawing room*."

Violet flinched at the logic. He was right, she was wrong. "I—"

Jack cleared his throat, and she stopped. There wasn't really an apology she could make for putting herself in danger. She should have taken his worry into account. She should have gotten him to go with her. It would have taken one moment to knock on the door and ask him to come with her.

Violet's head cocked as she examined Celia and Leopold.

"Just *what* are you trying to say, Wakefield?" Leopold asked again.

"He seems like a man in love," Violet told Jack, examining Leopold. "I know that gaze."

"Or a man obsessed." Jack reached down to take her hand. "It's not that large of a step from love to obsession, Vi."

"What are you trying to say?" Leopold repeated.

"Men in love are prone to murder," Jack told Leopold. "We're disgusting animals, really."

Celia squeaked. Her gaze was wide and worried, and Violet had to wonder if she feared the man next to her or someone else?

# CHAPTER THIRTEEN

Celia hurried away without a comment, and Violet glanced at Jack, winked, and followed.

"Wait! Celia, wait!"

The girl slowed, glancing back. Her eyes were a deep brown and shining with tears. Violet rushed ahead, grabbing her wrist.

"It was Melrose you loved?"

She shook her head.

"Leopold?"

She shook her head again. Violet fought the desire to shake the girl. You didn't get to be cagey in your replies when you were discussing murder. The idea that somehow your secrets were your own in a murder investigation infuriated Violet. Didn't the dead deserve better? Didn't the living deserve the killer to be found?

"They both pursued you? Both brothers?"

Celia pressed her lips together, blinking rapidly. "For a while, Leopold pursued me. I thought this was it. Love. Finally. Finally I'd found it."

Violet nodded. "I understand. It seems impossible until it happens to you. Then it's magical."

"Except it wasn't for me. It all fell apart." A tear slipped down

Celia's cheek. "Leopold moved on to an American heiress, and the next thing I knew Melrose was pursuing me. He was so romantic. He brought me flowers. Not just zinnias—he brought me orchids. He wrote me poetry. He actually sang to me in front of my friends. I thought, this *must* be love. Leopold had thrown me over, but fate had saved me for something even better."

She sniffed, and Violet wrapped her arm around Celia's shoulders. This wasn't a happy ever after. It ended with a body that had been both poisoned and stabbed. Could Celia have done that? The girl didn't seem to be the kind to grab an ice pick and thrust it into the chest of someone she had loved.

"I was so happy," Celia continued. "I didn't think I could be that happy. Then—then—one of their previous victims found me. She told me about how Leopold and Melrose had done it to her. She showed me letters. They were the same as the ones I was cherishing. Word for word except our names. So, I decided, I'm going to confront them."

Violet tugged Celia towards a stone bench near the roses. It was cold outside, and she'd normally have brought Celia in for warm tea, but Vi didn't want the tale interrupted.

"Their man's half day is on Wednesday afternoons. So, I thought I could confront them without an audience. Servants know everything, and they talk. Maybe I'd even find the proof first—show it to them and make them tell me."

"How did you get them to talk to you?"

Celia bit her lip. "They didn't. I took Melrose's key from his coat. We had gone for a walk, and I pretended to be cold. He put his coat around me, and I took his key right out of his pocket."

Violet laughed. "I like how you work. What happened?"

"I let myself in. They almost always lunch at their club, so I knew I had time. I went through their desks. They have a log. An *actual* log! Of their conquests! Of points they assign for things!"

"Like what?"

Celia blinked rapidly as though fighting her tears. She sniffed, swallowed, and said without inflection, "Accepted proposals. Taking someone's ah—"

"Virginity?" Violet bit her bottom lip as she listened. "Were you in that log?"

"Not for that!" Celia's gaze darted to the side, and Violet didn't bother to argue. No one in their right mind would admit to such a thing.

"So you found your proof and you confronted them?"

Celia took in a slow breath. Tears were shining in her eyes, and she shook her head as she glanced away. "I was too much of a coward. They came back while I was there."

Violet gasped and Celia bit her lip. Her gaze was still fixed on the ground as though she'd found a treasure in the greenery. She told the flowerbeds, "I was so scared. I panicked, and I jumped into the coat closet. Thankfully, the Nelson brothers are too spoiled to hang up their own coats."

Violet laughed. Not so much at the statement, but at the snide disgust in Celia's voice.

"They were talking about their register. They give more points if the second brother can step in successfully as Melrose did with me."

"Oh my." Violet didn't see why Celia had ever walked or talked with the brothers again.

"I couldn't believe it. But, they were so cold, they were laughing. Over other girls. Over me. Over their great aunt who kept changing her will for them."

"So why are you *here?*"

"Kyle," Celia groaned. "You're rich! Kyle needs the money. Father wouldn't leave me at home alone."

Violet groaned. "My goodness, do these men have no shame? My money and I are *not* there for the taking. Why would anyone really think so?"

Celia's brow wrinkled. "Your mother," she said flatly. "Lady Eleanor made it seem as though you were desperate to marry. Father said we had to take the risk. He has had a series of bad investments, and well—things don't look good for Kyle or Father."

"But you'll be fine?"

"You're not the only one with an aunt."

Violet snorted. She noticed Jack walking past. She had little doubt that he'd keep Violet within view. Did he believe Celia was the killer? Violet would think so if it were only poisoning. And not because she believed poison was a woman's way to murder. Anyone who didn't want to get their hands dirty would use poison. Violet just didn't see Celia lashing out in a fury. She'd *hid* in the closet of the brothers' rooms if her story was to be believed.

"So then," Violet asked, "you were here with them. And thought you'd give them another chance. To see—"

"No!" Celia was trembling. "Melrose promised me, he *promised* that this time it was real. How could I believe him? I'd *heard* him laughing with Leopold. Their competition, Violet, it extends to *everything*. Who is inheriting from their great aunt. Who is the favourite son. Who has had the most women. But, Melrose said it was time for the games to end. It was time to stop being children. He said that he was in love, and it was real, and that he would spend the rest of his life making it up to me."

Violet pasted a commiserating expression on her face. Did Celia realize how her story sounded?

"Did you believe him?" Violet hoped that she hadn't, but someone had walked with the man in the garden so often that Cook had taken note.

Celia wiped away another tear. "How do you know if someone loves you? *Why* do you believe that Mr. Wakefield loves you? He probably doesn't. He probably only wants your money or your virtue."

Celia was so in earnest that Vi felt as though she had to answer. "You can never truly be sure when someone is lying to you or not. But—"

Celia's expression demanded Violet to come up with some way of explaining it all. Violet pushed her hair behind her ear as she gathered her thoughts. What she wouldn't give for a cup of Turkish coffee.

"There are the other factors. Jack hates that I put myself in danger, but he doesn't try to box me in."

Celia scoffed. "He doesn't want you to leave him. He wants your money. I've heard that rumor that he has money of his own, but if he gets yours, he'll still be able to prose on about how he won. It'll be *points* in the games that men play with each other."

"My money is pretty well and truly tied up. Jack won't benefit all that much from what I have."

"To other men, it will seem like he does. It's about the look of it, isn't it? Who won? Who gets your virtue? Who gets you to believe their lies?"

Violet took a long breath in. "You can tell if they're being straight with you by their fruits."

Celia blinked and then sputtered, "What?"

"By their fruits, you shall know them. Do you understand?"

"I had the love songs, the poems, the orchids. I had fruits, and they were all lies!"

"I don't know," Violet told Celia. "I know Jack loves me because he's protective, because he's kind, because he listens, he reads the books that I love. He sometimes finds me infuriating, but he's patient. He worries and then acts on those worries, so I'm safer. When he has a chance to choose between me and something else, he chooses me."

Celia's mouth twisted, and her expression said that Violet was wrong.

"My heart knows," Violet said flatly, and it did. She had no doubts that Jack loved her and would love her even if she were penniless.

"I thought my heart knew!"

"I'm sorry." Violet looked at the girl, the way her jaw was tight with fury, her eyes were flashing yet filled with tears. Her chest was heaving with pent up feelings. The poor, sad thing.

"It's not fair. I don't think love is real at all. Maybe a mother loves her child. Anything else? It's just a fairy story."

Violet rubbed the back of her neck. There was no talking Celia out of her theory, and Violet didn't feel like the truth Celia needed to hear was that she break with the surviving brother.

"You need to stay away from Leopold Nelson," she said anyway.

"I thought he loved me once," Celia said. "I had no doubts. Maybe he did. Maybe it isn't a fairy story." She wiped a tear away and admitted, "I don't want it to be all fairy tales and nonsense."

"Maybe he did love you. Maybe he realized what his brother was starting up again, and he thought—enough was enough. Maybe he killed his brother."

Celia gasped. "No. It must have been a tramp."

"A tramp?"

"Some homeless person passing through who tried to break in. That's far more reasonable than someone we *know*."

Perhaps, Vi thought, Celia was the victim of the cruel brother because she was out and out stupid. Violet squeezed Celia's hand and stood.

"My friend," Violet told her, "no. Of course it wasn't a tramp. The person who killed Melrose Nelson is someone staying in the house."

Celia gasped.

"Someone you know. Someone you have had dinner with and whom you've associated with. Possibly even someone you thought you once loved."

"That can't be true. They're *brothers*."

"My cousin murdered our great-aunt for an increase in income. Isolde's first betrothed was murdered by his own son. I'm not an expert in investigation like Jack is, but if I were going to guess on a killer, I would start my theories with family members."

Celia cried out, and Violet wanted to shake the girl. Celia truly was stupid. She was a target for the Nelson brothers because she was easily fooled. How many other women had they tried to play their games with and the woman had simply removed them from her life and moved on with those who were far more trustworthy?

Violet took Celia's hand. "There are good people in the world and bad people, and often others don't react the way we think they will or the way that they should. We're not characters on a page, and love isn't only flowers and songs. Life can be quite messy."

Celia gaped and hurried away, saying over her shoulder, "You're wrong."

# CHAPTER FOURTEEN

Jack was a dark figure in the shadows of the house. Violet wasn't sure that Celia had even noticed him. Violet knew, however, that it was an assumption she shouldn't make. Celia had been forward thinking enough to steal a key and dig through the Nelson brothers' rooms—if she could be trusted. If what Celia had said was true, the woman had motive for murder as clear and obvious as any motive Violet had ever seen.

Violet crossed to Jack, who watched her come with an even expression. "Shall we elope?"

Jack leaned down while he lifted her chin. "I love you, Violet, and if you think that I will not watch you walk down the aisle and take my name in front of everyone we know, you are very wrong."

His voice was so possessive that Violet shivered. She had to pause and compare her need for freedom to her absolute willingness to be Jack's. Perhaps when you were possessive in return, it wasn't stifling?

Vi grinned at him, noting that strong jaw and those penetrating eyes. "Have you been thinking about the wedding day?"

"Well...I've been thinking about a portion of the day." His grin was wicked as he kissed her brow once more, and she shivered again. "So, let's not let it get stolen from us by getting murdered along with Melrose."

She heard his simple scold and knew he needed—deserved—a reply. "I should have knocked on the door to get you before I followed Celia."

"True." He rubbed his chin over the top of her head, and she felt him breathe her in.

It was moments like this one, Violet thought, that made you believe in love. "They were playing a game. Those cruel brothers." Violet pulled back to look at him. "They were competing with each other."

"For what?"

"Everything. Most of all, however, for who could gather someone's affections better. It sounded like it was usually women, but maybe it was anyone or anything. Celia mentioned their great aunt's will, a woman's virtue, protestations of love from fools like Celia."

"That's a pretty strong motive for murder." Jack's words illustrated Violet's opinion perfectly.

"Maybe," Vi said. "Celia. Perhaps Leopold. Perhaps Celia's father or brother if they knew what the brothers had been doing to Celia. I could even see another victim with a reason for murder, along with anyone who might have loved a victim."

"You don't think Celia was the killer?"

"I can't see her meeting him in the drawing room where anyone could have seen her and then stabbing him with an ice pick."

Jack tugged on Violet's hand and they headed towards the house. "It was a bloody scene. I can't see any woman having done that, but sometimes we don't desire to see the truth in front of us."

Violet caught sight of her brother, Geoffrey, in the window watching her and Jack. He didn't even pretend he wasn't spying on them. She stared pointedly at him, and he shot her a smirk and dropped the curtain he'd pulled back.

Violet glanced at Jack, but he was turned the other way. She wasn't sure if she should point out her brother, but she decided against it. He was already a wart, and it would be better if Jack didn't despise Violet's little brother. She could despise him for the both of them.

"I'm ready for some nosh, darling. Cook made an excellent dinner. How is she on breakfast?"

They opened a side door into the house and walked towards the breakfast room.

"What were you doing outside? It is very untoward to find you two sneaking around." Lady Eleanor's voice cut through the hall, and Jack and Violet turned to face her stepmother. "I don't approve of your engagement, and I will do all in my power to stop this wedding."

Violet could feel Jack's arm turned to stone.

"There is no scenario," Violet told her stepmother, "where I leave the money Aunt Agatha left me to Geoffrey."

Lady Eleanor blinked rapidly. She seemed to actually be speechless, which was a state Violet didn't think possible.

"Geoffrey was not related to Aunt Agatha," Violet continued, "and she would not approve of leaving the money outside of her family unless I were leaving it to a charity."

"Once the money was willed, it became available for you to leave how you choose," Lady Eleanor snapped.

"The money is currently willed to Victor and a variety of charities," Violet lied. It was partly willed to Isolde, but Lady Eleanor would never give up ruining things for Violet and Jack if that became common knowledge. "Once I have children, the money will be fully left to them."

Also a lie as Violet had every intention of leaving money to Victor's children as well. Aunt Agatha never should have divided it un-evenly between them.

"We'll be married in April," Violet told her stepmother, and Jack stilled even more so. She glanced up at him and then back to her stepmother, hoping he was happy with the date. "We're going to have a big wedding, with a white dress and everybody we know. Come if you'd like. We'll send you an invitation."

Lady Eleanor gaped as Violet turned to Jack. "I'm ready for the whole breakfast. Roasted tomatoes, fried bread, beans, eggs, bacon, sausage, ham, all of it. Then I think I'll sleep off my breakfast."

"Maybe we should have a wedding breakfast after a morning

wedding." Jack suggested, his gaze almost hot on her face. He kissed her gently on the lips before tucking her hand on his elbow again.

Violet grinned at Lady Eleanor's gasp.

"Are you ignoring me?" Lady Eleanor would have probably thumped her cane if she had one. "I do *not* approve of this wedding. Or, for that matter, your intent to overindulge on breakfast."

Vi laughed.

Lady Eleanor, however, continued. "We have guests, and you have a responsibility to them."

"Are you referring to the gentlemen you invited to distract me from Jack? To ruin things between me and my love so that I could marry some poor but well-connected man?" Lady Eleanor paused and started to reply, but Violet lifted a hand. "I realize that you don't approve of Jack. I don't need you to approve of him. I realize that you don't care for my behavior. Normally, I would say that you are absolutely right to find my behavior unacceptable. However, I find that I am ill-inclined to play nice with the gentlemen you brought to replace Jack."

She gasped, grabbing her throat in the shock. "You are the daughter of an earl! You can do better!"

"You have the worst taste in gentlemen of anyone I have ever seen, and my best friend is married to the laziest man I know. He might be lazy, but he's a good man. You can't say that of most of the men you've thrown into my or Isolde's lives."

"How dare you speak to me that way!"

"Danvers was a criminal whose fortune was fake."

"Tomas is a good man."

"*Victor and I* sent Tomas to Isolde, knowing he'd love her. You had nothing to do with Tomas. You do, however, have quite a bit to do with the men here. Theodophilus Smythe-Hill manipulates idiots like Algernon into betting their fortunes. He blackmails them."

"He's the nephew of a baron!"

"His birth doesn't matter! He's as much of a criminal as Danvers!"

"Algernon probably lied to you."

"Theodophilus tried to hurt me."

"You probably teased him."

Violet closed her eyes against the hurt. This—*this*—creature was what Vi could claim for a mother.

"The Nelson brothers were playing games with Celia Rosens's affections and countless others. Theodophilus, whether you want to believe it or not, is a blackguard. I'll admit that Lord Devonsly is a good man, but he's not for me. *Jack* is for me. Make your peace with it, or I'll call Father down on you."

"Your father is on my side."

"Father gave Jack his blessing to ask for my hand," Violet told her quietly.

Lady Eleanor gasped.

"The days of you manipulating myself, my twin, or Isolde is over. I won't let you anymore." Violet's voice was calm and even. The emotion of their argument had faded and all that was left was a solemn promise.

"How dare you speak to me that way!"

"How dare you attempt to ruin my relationship with my love to marry me off to men who—what? Promised that they'd see Geoffrey was taken care of?"

Lady Eleanor's expression was all that Violet needed to confirm her guess.

"Geoffrey is the son of an earl," Violet said. "He's not stupid. He's being educated. He'll receive an allowance and probably won't have to work unless he wishes to live lavishly."

"He deserves better."

"Not from me," Violet said, turning away from Lady Eleanor. "My hunger has faded," she said to Jack.

"It will return when you smell the bacon," he said gently. After they had left Lady Eleanor's quiet tears behind, Jack asked, "Are you all right?"

Violet glanced up at him and admitted, "No. It's not like she's ever been a mother to me, but I don't stop wanting to have one."

"Vi, you did in Agatha. You know you did."

She nodded and tried for a brave smile, though his expression told her she hadn't succeeded. "I suppose I need to sleep a bit better. I feel like that was far more melodramatic than it would have been if I had slept well last night."

# CHAPTER FIFTEEN

Violet had long since come to the conclusion that breakfast was not her favourite meal of the day. Her favourite meal of the day was tea. Cucumber sandwiches, bite-sized cakes, muffins, and tea. Glorious tea. Sometimes coffee. Occasionally, she and Victor decided upon champagne.

This morning, however, after her night, her bad dreams, hearing Celia's terrible tale, and arguing with her stepmother in the hall like some sort of fishwife—she had built up an appetite that queued into place as soon as she smelled the bacon.

Violet loaded her plate of a size to rival Jack's, and he laughed as she ate it. The main problem with breakfast was that they only had regular coffee instead of the Turkish coffee Violet enjoyed.

She took a deep breath in and placed a hand over her stomach. It hurt a little but in the best way.

Jack laughed at Violet's groan. "We need to talk to the younger Rosens. Leopold as well."

She wanted to nap, and to be honest, she wanted Jack to nap with her. She wasn't sure she could sleep alone, not with the scent of blood in her nose and the memory of falling over Melrose Nelson's body in her mind. Though, Violet didn't think he was much of napper.

"What's all this?" Denny demanded. "Lila is still sleeping. She says you cry while you sleep. That's ruining my happy mood today, Vi. It's murderer capturing day, Vi, and I hear you are weepy."

"You cry while you sleep?" Jack asked with a tone that made Violet flinch.

Violet suddenly realized she should have told him about her problem. "Not all the time. Just after Jeremiah. And not every day."

"Where is everyone else?" she asked Denny.

"We are, apparently, the only ones callous enough to want breakfast after someone was murdered." Jack's smooth, even voice still somehow conveyed a hint of rage.

"Nah. Kate is sicking up. Victor is hovering. Beatrice too. Lila is sleeping off your bad dreams. Otherwise, they'd be callous enough too. Isolde and Tomas are probably escaping the madhouse in each other's eyes."

"Oh my," Violet laughed and then groaned at the pain in her stomach.

Denny made a plate while Violet sighed over her cup of too-weak coffee. "Poor Kate. Sick even before breakfast. I suppose we must clear our names and escape this house."

"Don't do the chalkboard thing without me," Denny said over his plate. "Or perhaps I should just carry this to my room."

Violet shook her head. "You're safe. I need to check on Isolde and Kate." She rose and glanced at Jack. "Would you walk with me?"

Jack followed Violet out of the breakfast room with Denny giggling and muttering about someone being in trouble. Vi looked around the hall ensuring it was empty. "I owe you an apology. A lot of them."

Jack's head tilted as Violet placed her hand on his. "We should have announced our engagement. That we didn't is my fault. That we're here is my fault. I'm failing at all of this, especially at loving you. I should have told you I've been having bad dreams."

Jack wove his fingers through hers. "I didn't tell you about Emily either, Vi. You accepted that far easier than I would have. Or did when it was Tomas, and you cared far less for Tomas than I did for Emily. Yet, I nearly ruined us over Tomas. We are, *both of us,* learning how to be something different together."

Violet pressed her face into Jack's chest. "I don't want to ruin what we have. I feel like I should know already how to be part of something with you because of Victor—"

"You never had to learn how to be with Victor, Vi. That was simply your life."

"Mr. Wakefield?" Inspector Wright interrupted. Violet sighed into Jack's chest and stepped away from him. That was an official query. Had someone discussed protocol with Inspector Wright? Violet guessed the tightness around his eyes and mouth said that someone farther up the chain of his command had heard from their superior.

"I'll go check on Kate and Isolde," Violet told Jack, knowing she wouldn't be welcome for whatever came next.

"Be safe, Vi. Use all your wits. Whoever killed Melrose is in the house."

She nodded.

With Kate throwing up, Violet wanted to go to her first, but Victor was there. Violet hurried up the stairs towards the family wing. Isolde's room was at the end of the hall, overlooking the rose gardens. Violet knocked on the door, and Tomas opened it.

"Oooh la la." Violet laughed. "Is Isolde sicking up too?"

"Ah." Tomas cleared his throat. "This isn't what it looks like."

Isolde peeked around Tomas's shoulder.

Violet winked at her little sister. "My goodness, where is your mother? Does she know of such goings on? Scandal! I declare scandal, scandal!"

"Are you all right?" Isolde asked. "I heard that you found the body."

Violet nodded. "Where were you when it happened?"

"Geoffrey, Gerald, and I went to play billiards," Tomas said. "Someone told your stepmother that Isolde was afraid of marrying me, so Isolde was dragged to a certain boudoir for a scold."

Violet laughed, patting Tomas on the cheek. "Who would do such a thing?"

"You would." Isolde tugged Tomas to the side and took Violet's hand.

Violet frowned. "So you were with Mama dearest. You boys were together. Other than Father, you have alibis. That's good. Has the good inspector asked you about things yet?"

Isolde and Tomas both nodded. "He was quite accusatory. Tomas yelled at the inspector."

Violet laughed, but it was more what was expected than how she truly felt. There was a part of her who was glad to know that the inspector was accusatory with everyone. If it were just her, she'd have significantly more to worry over. Violet's eyes filled with tears, and she hugged Isolde.

"I love you, Isolde. I'm glad you are back. Stay close to Tomas."

"Vi!" Isolde said as Violet started to hurry away. "What are you going to do?"

"Do?" Violet grinned back over her shoulder and shrugged.

"Be careful, Violet!"

She hurried down the servant's staircase to avoid the guests. None of them would know their way through the back stairs. The constables might have a servant to help them through the house, but the guests wouldn't.

Vi went through the kitchens and stopped to talk to Cook.

"Tell me straight," Violet said. "Who was Celia walking out with?"

Cook didn't answer, and Violet sighed. "I think you can do better than asking me like this."

"Are you trying to get a bribe?"

"Get out of here, girls," Cook said to the maids. "Lady Vi and I are going to have a chat."

Violet grinned as the maids scattered. They had been peeling potatoes and forming bread, but they left without even looking back. Violet picked up the knife, tossed it, and then caught it.

"You remember how to do that?"

"You didn't let me hide in the kitchens unless I learned to peel potatoes."

"Being a lady doesn't make you useless when I'm around."

Violet laughed as she worked the peel off of the potato. There was something so soothing about the slow pull of the knife against the vegetable. She did love a good roasted potato. Salt, pepper, onions. It would be lovely with a roasted chicken, perhaps some parsnips and carrots. Given how loaded her stomach was from breakfast, Violet wasn't quite sure why she was thinking so longingly of a roasted dinner.

"Who has Celia Rosens been walking with in the garden?"

"Did I miss how you followed her out one day?"

"I was eavesdropping then, not trying to solve a murder!"

Cook laughed. She kept stirring the pot on the stove.

"Fine! What do you want?"

"A holiday."

Violet tilted her head.

"You're rich now, Violet, and I'm tired."

Violet frowned. Cook had aged in the years since she'd taught Violet to peel the potatoes. Her eyes were heavily lined around the corners with laughter marks. Her skin was a little yellower than usual. Violet frowned, realizing that the sass had hidden a slowness.

"I want Jones to go as well. I think I'm sick, Lady Vi. I want to see a blue ocean and feel the sun on my face and spend an entire day just sitting next to the sea in a rocking chair."

"I would have done that for you regardless, Helena. I inherited a house on the Amalfi coast. It's lovely there. Warm. The sea is beautiful. Or Cuba? Victor and I really enjoyed Cuba."

"As long as the ocean is blue and the air is warm."

"I would have given you a trip without your information," Violet said gently.

"I know. You always were kind. It makes me feel better, though, to exchange something with you."

Violet nodded. "What can you tell me?"

"Celia Rosens walked out with all of them. Her father and her brother knew."

"All of them?"

Cook nodded. "Devonsly and both brothers. You know who else knew? Geoffrey. That boy lurks in the shadows and watches everything."

Violet shivered. Her brother needed to be removed from his mother's influence. She wasn't sure that doing something like that, however, was a forgivable offense.

"Who do you think killed Melrose?"

Cook shrugged. "I only make the food, Lady Vi."

"You hear every piece of gossip to come through this house."

Cook grinned. "That I do."

"What do the servants think?"

"They don't mind Kyle Rosens or Lord Devonsly."

Violet laughed. She had barely talked to Kyle Rosens, and though he'd come for her money, she didn't doubt the servants. She could understand needing money. Of course, when she had needed it more desperately, she'd picked up her pen and started writing novels. The kind that sold for next to nothing, but her portion added up to silk stockings and eggs.

She stretched her neck.

"Do you think that Celia is the type of girl to stab someone with an ice pick?"

"All I can say for sure," Cook replied with a grin, "is that you could."

Violet gasped, but when she finished peeling the potatoes, she took the tea that Cook offered and leaned back to sip.

"You aren't offended?"

Violet shook her head. "I wouldn't hurt someone for money or for anything like that. I think that's the question. I don't have any reason to have hurt Melrose Nelson. You can ask me, you, Isolde. Any of us—we don't have a motive to have killed the man. So who does?"

"That girl Celia. Her family. Possibly her brother. Perhaps even Lord Devonsly, depending on how he felt about her."

Violet nodded and reached out, taking Cook's hand. "Give your notice, take the chance at the Amalfi coast. You and Mrs. Jones have enough to see you through your illness there."

"I don't think I'll be getting better, Lady Vi. Jones doesn't have enough savings, even with mine, to survive through her old age."

Violet nodded at the unspoken plea. "You don't know what life will bring for you, or how long you'll survive if you're not working from dawn past dusk. Either way, Mrs. Jones will be fine."

"It's so much easier to ask for help for others rather than ourselves. Violet, I see the dark circles under your eyes."

"It's hard being here," Violet admitted. "It's hard after the last few years. Aunt Agatha. The poor souls who've died. My memories chase me through my dreams, and they're never kind. I spend so many nights unable to sleep. I can't help but look at myself and think about how weak I am. All around us are lads who saw so much worse in the trenches, fighting to keep people like *me* safe. I can't even—"

Cook shook her head. "Their suffering doesn't negate yours, Lady Vi."

"I see dead eyes when I close mine. Dead eyes staring at nothing."

"We all die, Lady Violet. They died earlier than they wanted. It's a burden I have been thinking a lot about. Don't spend so much of your life suffering for the dead that you forget to live."

"What am I supposed to do?"

"Go find that man of yours and tell him."

Violet shook her head. "He is so much stronger than I am. I don't want him to think I'm weak."

"Burdens are so much easier when they're shared. I can assure you that no honorable man wants to watch his love suffer. Cherish that man of yours by letting him help you."

Violet set down her teacup and stood. She pressed a kiss to Cook's cheek. "I think you'll like the Amalfi coast."

"Is the water blue?"

Vi nodded.

"Is the air warm?"

Vi nodded.

"Jones will be there?"

Vi nodded.

"Then it sounds like heaven."

"A little piece of it anyway," Violet told her.

"That's all I've ever wanted," Cook replied. Violet squeezed her hand lightly and left. She had to fight back tears as she hurried up the servant staircase to the wing where she and her friends had been isolated. Without Mrs. Jones and Cook, the house would lose much of its appeal.

## CHAPTER SIXTEEN

The servant staircase was the most effective way to move through houses like the earl's. It was intended to get the person from the starting point to their end point with little fuss. There would be no strolling down these stairs, hand on the railing, while a ball gown floated around a spoiled daughter. Therefore, one could do things like pulling a skirt up a little higher to dart up the stairs.

Tears were burning at the back of Violet's eyes, and she was very much afraid that the kindness she'd just extended to Cook would end as Cook expected—with the final days of her life.

Violet stepped out of the hallway near her bedroom and stopped in her tracks. If it wasn't Theodophilus Smythe-Hill and if he didn't have his hands on Beatrice.

Violet's hands clenched into fists, and she marched down the hallway, ignoring the lush carpets, the portraits of ancestors of previous generations intermixed with pieces of art from grandmasters.

"What's all this?" Violet asked in forced cheer. She took hold of her maid and pulled her free from Theo's grasping hands. Out of the corner of her eye, Violet saw Beatrice rub above her elbow.

"I made a simple request, and she didn't comply. You know, I saw her coming out of my bedroom. I wonder if anything is missing."

"Did you? And then you followed her to this wing? Your bedroom isn't anywhere near here." Violet smiled prettily. "Let's call my father, the earl, shall we? He'll have her searched. I assume it was just now?"

Theo's gaze narrowed on Violet. "I'm sure it was nothing. I'll let you know if something is missing."

"No, no," Violet shook her head. "No. She'll come with me. I'll search her. We'll clear this up immediately."

Theo's snake-like smile appeared. "Perhaps you should rid yourself of the wench. Good help is so hard to find. Thieves and sneaks—better to not have a maid at all."

"Lady Violet—"

Vi winked at Beatrice with the eye turned away from Theo, and then cocked her head at the man.

"You're not housed on this floor."

"Just a bit lost."

"Let me help you," Violet said merrily, though her insides were roiling. "Fortune-hunting, money-grubbers have the smaller rooms towards the back of the house."

His expression hardened, and he stepped up, taking her shoulders. "Do you think you're better than me because some idiot slaughtered that old woman you called an aunt? Flattering a stupid, old, unwanted woman into leaving her fortune to you doesn't make you saint. You stole that money from John Davies and Algie. From your own twin."

Violet's mind skipped around with all of her options.

"You let go of Lady Vi." Beatrice yanked at Theo's arm but couldn't get his grip to loosen.

"Or what?" Theo snarled and turned again on Violet. "You think that stepmother of yours will believe you *over me?* Lady Eleanor has been friends with my mother since before you were born. She is actually fond of me. Unlike you, the unwanted, unnecessary spawn of a wife who couldn't survive the influenza? Weak. Useless and unwanted. Like mother, like daughter."

"You know," Violet said, looking up at Theo. "You really do sound like a snake." She stepped into him, further elucidating her feelings with a swift, sharp knee to his manhood. Theo choked, grabbing himself and falling to his knees.

"Bravo!" Victor called. "Bravo, Vi. Perfectly executed. Jack will be so proud."

Violet shot her brother a quelling look. Had he been watching the show? She looked down at Theo and realized she was rather glad Victor had let her get her revenge. She was much less afraid of him now, groaning on the floor, than she had been that morning. She reached out blindly for Beatrice and said to Victor, "I'll leave this mess to you. I find I am not opposed to further violence."

Violet glanced beyond Victor to Kate, noting the dark circles under her eyes. "Are you all right, love?"

"Tip-top," Kate lied, looking at anything but Violet.

Vi frowned. "Come, Beatrice. I believe my brother left something fortifying in my bedroom after last night. Let's share a cup, shall we, and relive the conquest of the villain."

The maid followed blindly, her gaze still fixed on Theo as though she couldn't quite believe they had freed themselves. Theo, however, was eyeing Victor with a combination of fear and disdain. Oh how she hated this man, but she did adore that look on his face. "Do call Jack this time, Victor. Perhaps a little bonding over bloody knuckles will be good in the long term."

Victor grinned as Theo paled even further—a sight that pleased her to no end.

Violet was sipping her small glass while she stared at the chalkboard. Poor Beatrice had cried once Violet pushed her into a chair and handed her a glass of whisky.

Victor really did love slopping it into tea whenever Violet looked as though she might cry. She grinned at the memories of him thrusting a cup of tea at her and begging her to drink, not cry. It never did work. Her poor twin.

Violet's thoughts tripped back to the last time she'd seen Theo at the nightclub. He truly was a fool. It wasn't as though Victor hadn't told Theo to stay away from Violet, yet he'd appeared at their home. Did he truly believe that Lady Eleanor had so much power over the twins? The best that Violet could hope for as far as Theo's brain capacity was that he hoped to slide into Isolde's affections.

Violet was afraid, however, that the truth was far more. That he thought he could tell her that she didn't understand what had happened last time he'd caught her alone. Maybe, rather like the Nelson brother, Theo assumed that Violet would forgive and forget. Especially with Lady Eleanor taking his part.

It didn't say much for Theo's capacity to understand women, but it wouldn't be a surprising revelation either. Violet had very, very little respect for the average man and his capacity to understand women. Perhaps also, Violet thought, she had very little respect for too many women who were still allowing themselves to be controlled and trapped by the expectation men put on them. Men or stepmothers.

She stared at her glass, wishing for a moment that it was ginger wine and then shuddering as the memories of ginger wine returned.

"My lady, I feel quite lazy."

"My dear Beatrice," Violet countered. "I fully expect you to take the rest of the day off. In fact, why don't you take Lila's maid and go to the kitchens. You can send Lila's girl up with a large tea tray for our chalkboard work. The two of you can gather up Jack and our friends and then return to the kitchens. Mrs. Jones and Cook need information about traveling to the Amalfi Coast."

Beatrice nodded, setting down the whisky glass with a look of distaste, and hurried towards the door. She seemed relieved to have something to do. It was a feeling Violet could understand. Her own bad memories seemed to get her when she was least expecting it, but it always helped if she had something to keep her focus.

Speaking of things to keep her focus, Violet looked at the list of names on the board. She considered Melrose Nelson. Her own experience with him was limited indeed. She needed...perhaps she needed her little brother. She blinked rapidly at the idea. Cook had said he was an unrepentant wart who spied on everyone. Just what did he know?

Her mouth twisted, and she sent for her brother. As she waited for everyone to appear, Violet adjusted the board to her liking and arranged the chairs so that they were bordering the bed. She then updated the board:

. . .

MELROSE NELSON —VICTIM

- Both stabbed and poisoned. Was he hated so much that someone needed to be absolutely certain he was dead? Or, perhaps worse, was he a victim twice over?
- The Nelson brothers played a points-system game with each other that manipulated the people in their lives. Celia Rosens was one of the victims. Was anyone else in the house affected by their behavior? Surely that was a reason to murder someone, but who was driven that far?

LEOPOLD NELSON —BROTHER

- Leopold is a snake, as is his brother. Either of them could have been murdered for the same reasons. Perhaps Melrose drove his brother to the edge of murder first?

LORD DEVONSLY

- Seemed to believe that Carlyles wouldn't need to murder anyone. Did that extend to himself? He is also aristocratic.
- Walked out with Celia. Perhaps he was in love? Perhaps he heard her story and was driven to murder?

SIR ROSENS—FATHER

- His daughter was romanced and heartbroken by Melrose Nelson. Did vengeance come into play? If so, is Leopold next?

KYLE ROSENS—BROTHER

- Would this brother kill for his sister?

CELIA ROSENS

- Melrose had been walking with Celia in the gardens. But so had Lord Devonsly and Leopold. Could jealousy have driven someone to kill Melrose? Celia had been manipulated by the brothers. Perhaps she'd had enough? Perhaps she thought that Leopold wouldn't return unless Melrose was dead?

Violet cleared her throat as she examined the board. She erased the names of her family. Most of them had alibis and none of them had a motive. She stepped away from the board.

"I had heard," Denny started, but Violet gasped and whirled. She grabbed her stomach and stared. Somehow while Vi had been making notes, her friends had arrived with Father and Geoffrey, and everyone had seated themselves.

"You *are* tired," Lila said. "I thought you were focused and didn't want to interrupt your thoughts with greetings, but Vi, love, you must rest."

"What's wrong with Violet?" Father leaned back with tea that Kate had poured for him. Had they really been getting tea and watching her? She blinked rather stupidly at them and realized things were worse than she had thought.

"She's not sleeping," Lila told the earl. "It might be time to travel to the sea again."

"After all this is over, she can curl up in her childhood home and find some peace." Father adjusted his jacket while everyone else paused and stared at him. He cleared his throat as every set of eyes dropped.

"Father," Victor said as delicately as possible, "the sea might be a better choice."

"Mmm, the sound of waves is relaxing," Violet added, to let her father escape his mistake with grace.

She stepped back, pouring herself a cup of coffee. She took a deep breath in and closed her eyes in sheer joy at the Turkish coffee. Just what she needed. She noted her brother's addition of chocolate liqueur on the cart and poured a little into her cup as well. Victor winked at Violet, and they both sipped from similarly doctored coffees.

Violet's gaze flicked over the group.

"Isolde?"

"She's distracting her mother," Victor said.

"Jack?"

"He's working with Inspector Wright, but he said Kyle and Sir Rosens have alibis for the time of the murder but not with each other. Sir Rosens had his man with him. Kyle and Theo were playing billiards."

Violet's expression made Victor laugh. "Jack had Theo brought to a local inn. He can't leave the area for now, but he won't be staying here."

"Why can't the boy stay here?" Father demanded. None of them answered, and he snorted a little, letting out a low grumble, but as a group, they abdicated explaining.

# CHAPTER SEVENTEEN

Violet paced in front of the chalkboard while Denny and Victor considered who had the greater reason to murder. She had replaced her slim gold band with her engagement ring. Violet rubbed her thumb over the stones, letting the sign of Jack's love comfort her while she paced.

"It doesn't make sense," Violet announced.

"Murder often doesn't," Father said.

She barely kept from shooting him an irritated expression. Murder didn't make sense to people who would never kill, but there was still a logic to it. There was a *reason* why someone killed. Even if the reason was never something that others would act on.

She went to the board and crossed out every name but Celia and Leopold. "Only these two make sense. At least these two who don't have alibis. You saw Celia with Leopold and Melrose?"

She turned to Geoffrey. The inner wart was hidden with Father present, and the boy nodded. He really did need to spend more time with Father, Violet thought. Her gaze flicked over her friends again. Denny was grinning like a loon while Lila seemed a bit bored.

Kate, on the other hand, looked as though she were trying not to sick up and Victor was watching his love like a hawk. Just how ill was she? If she was so very sick, why hadn't they sent for a doctor?

Father was watching Violet closely, as was—to Violet's surprise—Geoffrey.

"What doesn't make sense about Celia doing the killing?" Geoffrey asked. "If she can be believed, those brothers were playing games with her."

"Why didn't she attack them while she was in their home? She'd stolen the key. If she was so upset about their behavior, why didn't she poison their gin and then leave? No one would have ever expected her for such a crime." Violet paced, playing with her ring.

"I wouldn't have killed over that," Lila said, sipping her tea. She glanced at Violet and added, "You wouldn't either. If you realized that Jack was playing some sort of point game with you, you'd renounce him publicly, tell his story to that woman reporter, then catch a ship to somewhere exotic. I would have thrown a fit that left their ears ringing for decades and slapped them soundly, but murder?" Lila shrugged. "I can't see it. Kate, the mildest of us, would probably have said something scathing and then bought a new book."

Kate laughed, then placed her fingers over her mouth as though laughing had been a terrible mistake. Victor took her hand, weaving their fingers together. His eyes were dark with concern, and Violet realized her twin was hiding something from her. Why hadn't he said that Kate was ill? The murder? Concern for Vi and her lack of sleep? Whatever was going on?

"Well, murderers don't act like other people, right?" Geoffrey asked, glancing among them. "If deciding to kill someone were a regular sort of action, there would be a whole lot more bodies lying around."

There was enough of mockery in his tone to show that he felt they were missing all of the obvious clues.

"So Celia did walk out with both of them?" Violet asked the boy.

Geoffrey glanced at their father, flushed a little, and said, "I saw her with both brothers. Both brothers kissed her rather—ah—fervently."

The earl didn't react, but Violet had no doubt that he was

displeased to know his son was lurking in the bushes and at windows, watching people. Violet returned to pacing, playing with her ring.

"Poisoning someone is something you plan," Violet said. "I wonder if they've figured out what poison it was. Even if they know, discovering where it came from will be difficult if they aren't sure who did the poisoning."

"Why?" Geoffrey demanded.

"Because," Victor answered, "our guests came from all over. It's much easier to trace one person and the purchases they made than all of us and where we've been. For example, if they believed it was me, they would interview Violet, Mr. Giles, and all the places I stopped on the way to the homestead. They would check the chemists around my house in London. They could even put my picture in the newspaper and ask for information from chemists who may have sold me arsenic or whatever poison was used. They're only finalizing the case that way."

Violet listened to her brothers while she paced. She stopped in her tracks as she stared at the chalkboard.

"There's always a reason," she said. "Strong feelings like love or hatred. Greed. Self-defense. Even an accident."

She looked at Denny, who laughed. "You don't accidentally poison and stab someone."

"Agreed."

"You can rule out self-defense with the poison."

Violet nodded.

"These brothers aren't ones who love. Not with the games they play. I doubt they even love each other. Celia—maybe she loved them or maybe she avenged the way they played with her heart."

Violet turned to Geoffrey. "Did you lurk in the drawing room at all before we got here? Did you witness how they acted before the murder?"

Geoffrey shrugged.

"Speak boy," Father ordered without his composure slipping.

"A little."

"Did you see Melrose ever come into the room after everyone had left?"

"He liked to walk at night." Geoffrey glanced at his father again. "One time he got a book of poetry and was reading it aloud—as though he were practicing. I did hear them arguing once. The brothers were arguing about money. One of them hadn't paid a bill he should have or something."

Violet nibbled at her lip. She tilted her head at the board, but her mind was buzzing. She needed to sleep. She needed to curl up on her bed and let her mind hover over the possibilities. She was rather afraid, however, that she'd close her eyes and see Jeremiah Allen floating in the water again. Or perhaps she'd see Danvers's dead and staring eyes.

"Why did the other killers act?" Geoffrey asked. "That article made it seem like you were involved in a lot of cases."

Victor answered while Violet continued to pace. "Greed, hatred, obsession, pride, revenge."

Father finally rose. "I would like to finish my book. Victor, you should take your Kate back to her room before she gets sick all over Violet's. Later today, you should come and speak to me."

Victor nodded, his jaw clenching, and Violet blinked stupidly at both of them.

"I need to sleep," she announced. "I feel like my mind isn't even working. This is going to have to be a case solved by Jack and Inspector Wright. I'm useless."

Lila rose and dragged a complaining Denny from the room. "I wanted to watch her pin down the villain."

"She's not pinning down anything but her pillow," Lila told him. "Oh laddie, track down Jack and see if he'll tell you anything."

"He never tells me anything," Denny whined. "I might as well ask Vi's and Victor's dogs for information."

Violet lay down on her bed after her bedroom cleared. She stared towards the chalkboard, trying to sleep and failing. She finally got up and pulled out her journal to read over her thoughts from previous cases. She flipped back to the first case when she'd lost Aunt Agatha and read about when Violet had been an attempted murder suspect when someone had poisoned Aunt Agatha's regular nightly drink.

Violet sniffed, her fingers tracing the pages. Her worries for Aunt Agatha had been so intense at that moment. She'd wanted nothing more than for her aunt to escape the house and find safety somewhere else, anywhere else. Violet would have been happy to have had Aunt Agatha abandon the twins at that time to keep her alive.

Her wants, however, had not been taken into account, and Meredith had succeeded in poisoning their aunt. Violet curled onto her side, reliving the memory as she slipped into sleep.

~

"Violet?"

She slowly sat up. She hadn't expected to sleep, and she felt as though she could have slept for twenty minutes or two days. She blinked rapidly, rubbing her brow, and cleared her throat. "One moment."

She found Jack peeking into the bedroom. She rose, making her way to the bath, and splashed her face with water.

When Violet left her bath, Jack and Victor were standing in her bedroom.

"Shall we walk?"

Violet nodded, taking Jack's arm and going with him down the back stairs. "Inspector Wright arrested Celia Rosens."

Violet stared at Jack. "What?"

"She had arsenic in her bedroom."

Violet blinked and sniffed, laying her head against his arm. "That doesn't seem right."

"It seems unlikely that she'd have stabbed her former lover with an ice pick."

"What does Inspector Wright believe?"

"He believes that she was caught attempting to poison him and he attacked her. She was forced to defend herself."

"What about blood on her clothes?" Violet shuddered with the recollection of the blood she'd gotten on herself. There had been so much blood that Violet had been soaked. She didn't see how someone could have stabbed Melrose Nelson without getting it on themselves.

"Some of her things had been found burned."

Violet frowned. That—well—she supposed they must need to get her clothes out of the way. "But she didn't leave fingerprints on the ice pick?"

"It was wiped clean."

"I—" Violet shook her head. Celia had been thoroughly abused by Leopold *and* Melrose Nelson. Why then did only Melrose die? Violet would love to ask Celia and hear her justification, but Vi guessed it was a matter of being caught before she could finish the crime. Or perhaps it was simpler. Celia might have imagined that with Melrose gone, Leopold might stop his games. "They took her away already?"

"Her father and brother went along. They're interviewing her more thoroughly. I believe he'll be able to eventually get a confession even though she was swearing that she was innocent.

Violet rubbed her brow, remembering the certainty she'd felt that Celia wouldn't have been able to stab Melrose. Perhaps Violet had gotten too used to guessing the end of these crimes. She truly was baffled.

"Did Victor go talk to Father?"

Jack shook his head. "He seems genuinely upset by Kate being ill. I suspect that he's avoiding your father to hover over Kate."

Violet took in a deep breath and slowly let it out. "I suppose it's time to let this go."

"Tell me what's happening with you, Violet. Why am I only now hearing of your bad dreams?"

"I didn't want you to worry," Violet told Jack, knowing he'd hate the answer. "I am going to claim that I would have told you if I were thinking more clearly."

Jack pulled her to a stop. "The murderer has been found. What can I do to help? Do you want to go to the sea?"

Violet shrugged. "I think I might have to do the things that worked for Tomas. He walked a lot and wrote in his journal and focused on good things. Maybe I should increase my activity so I'm more likely to sleep hard."

Jack and Violet made their way to the stone bench where Violet had spoken to Celia. The dinner hour was approaching, and Violet was sure that she'd have to change and be kinder to her stepmother this time. It was important that she build bridges there if she could, especially after the argument in the hallway.

"I feel like I wouldn't have reacted as I did with Lady Eleanor if I weren't so tired. I feel like I would have seen that Celia *could* have killed Melrose if I'd be able to focus on her more. Why did she talk to me at all?"

Jack shook his head. They sat for a time and finally returned back inside to dress for dinner. He kissed her under the eaves near the door before they stepped an appropriate distance apart and went to their bedrooms.

# CHAPTER EIGHTEEN

Violet let Beatrice pick her dress, so when she placed her hand on the railing and let her dress float around her, it was a long swathe of red that matched her red lipstick and the light layer of rouge on her cheeks. Her eyebrows were penciled in, her lashes were darkened, and Violet was wearing her strand of black pearls and diamond bangles.

Jack waited for her at the bottom of the stairs with Kate and Victor next to him. Kate glowed with health, and Violet blinked at her. Her skin seemed to be shining and her eyes were alight with a sparkle that shocked Violet.

"I take it that I am not the only one who slept the afternoon away while Inspector Wright was solving the case?"

"I did indeed," Kate said. "Darling Beatrice woke me, and I felt like a whole new woman."

Violet kissed the air next to Kate's cheek to avoid leaving a smear of lipstick and then squeezed Victor's hand before taking Jack's arm.

"I should confess before we go into dinner that Lady Eleanor and I argued in the hall like fishwives fighting over the last fish."

Kate's head tilted and she frowned. "Do fishwives fight over fish?

Surely they don't. I feel like they must fight over the non-fish parts of their lives."

Violet grinned. "If fishwives do battle over fish, my dear step-mother and I re-enacted their fierce combat this morning. Keep your distance, darlings."

"Never," Kate swore.

Victor sighed. "We did miss out, my darling," he told Kate. To Violet, he said, "Perhaps tonight is the night we heavily indulge in my creations to dull our other senses."

Violet laughed and followed Victor to the bar in the parlor where they were gathering before dinner. Leopold Nelson had already arrived with a black armband tied on his bicep. With the Rosens family and Theodophilus Smythe-Hill no longer staying with them, the parlor was nearly entirely family. Leopold and Devonsly were the only remaining fortune hunters, but Violet wouldn't object to spending another weekend with Devonsly for a house party.

"Victor, my friend," Devonsly said cheerily, not putting on the more appropriate solemnity. "I wonder if you could make a drink for me too. I suppose the bottles were all examined? We're safe enough?"

Victor frowned. "Well actually—" He pulled out a bottle of gin, checking the seal. "Looks like every bottle is new." Victor ran his fingers over the bottles, pulling them out here and there to see what was available. "We're working fresh here, lads." He pulled out a familiar bottle of rum.

"Vi, love, Kate was wanting a rum cocktail. You?"

Vi nodded and watched as Devonsly and Leopold walked over to join Victor and Jack while the cocktails were made. Lila and Denny had yet to arrive in the parlor, so the first round of cocktails went to Devonsly, Violet, and Kate. Father watched carefully as Victor easily made several rounds of cocktails.

"I'll take an El Presidente as well," Jack told Victor. "I was thinking about our trip to Cuba this afternoon when the local boys took away the old bottles. One of the lads hadn't had rum before."

"More of a gin man, myself," Leopold said. "I find a good G&T to be just the thing before bed. Heard you had bad dreams, Vi. Maybe you should try my sleeping method."

Violet smiled and sipped her drink. She didn't reply. Celia may have committed the murder, but Vi did not care for Leopold. He and his brother were ultimately responsible for what had happened.

"Always best to try new things," Victor told Leopold, handing him an El Presidente. Violet was sure her twin had pushed the cocktail on Leopold simply because he wanted a G&T. Leopold frowned as he took the glass, sniffing at it like Victor might be attempting another round of poisoning.

"You sure you want a policeman?" Leopold joked as he faced Violet. "Jack here seems all right, but I wouldn't mind a rich wife."

"She's sure," Jack said flatly.

Leopold grinned while everyone else was trying to hide their shock. "I suppose my lot isn't so bad now that I don't have to share with Melrose, God rest his soul, but I say Wakefield, you're a lucky man to catch such a wealthy fish."

Violet looked at Kate to see if she'd misheard, but Kate was staring in shock at Leopold as well.

"That's an entirely inappropriate comment," Father told Leopold. "I imagine that you're struggling with the loss of your brother, and we can all appreciate your pain. Let me remind you that something terrible occurred here last evening, a young woman has been taken away for a terrible crime, and my poor wife and daughter are so bothered they are unable to leave their rooms."

While Father was chastising Leopold, Violet's oldest brother, Gerald, entered the room with Lila and Denny. Behind them was Isolde's betrothed, Tomas.

"Ah, yes, of course," Leopold said. "As you said, I'm out of sorts. Melrose. Well..." Leopold cleared his throat and blinked rapidly. It all seemed as though he were fighting his emotions, but Violet noted that his eyes had no shine and he had little trouble turning to the others. "Carlyle. Denny. Mrs. Denny."

Violet bit her bottom lip and looked again at Kate, who wasn't even trying to hide her shock.

"My apologies for your loss," Gerald told Leopold, shaking his hand. "Never been one for teetotalers, but your brother told a good story and I enjoyed speaking with him."

Violet reached out and took Kate's hand as Lila joined them, taking Violet's cocktail from her and sipping it before settling next to Vi.

"Next time," Lila said, "let's go someplace where emotions are less fraught. I feel certain we should have gotten your summons and boarded a ship to Monaco or back to Cuba."

She leaned back, grateful that Jack was leading Leopold away from her, and sighed. "I suppose that means my stepmother is not coming down to dinner."

Lila lifted the cocktail Denny handed her and saluted the news.

"We should leave tomorrow," Violet told the others. "This visit must end before more battle lines are drawn between Lady Eleanor and myself that end with things ruined between us."

Kate shifted, running her hand down her arms. "Victor and your father have an appointment tomorrow. We can see you back in London if you'd like to leave quickly."

"An appointment?"

She nodded but didn't elaborate. Vi glanced at Lila, who shrugged and sipped her cocktail. Violet turned back to Kate, who was deliberately looking the other way. Her feelings weren't hurt. Instead, she found herself running through the things that Victor and her father might talk about that he would keep from Vi. Only one thing came to mind. Her jaw dropped as she stared at Kate—everything clicking into place.

"By Jove!" Violet muttered, taking a rather large swallow of her cocktail.

"Hush," Kate said, blushing brilliantly.

Violet nodded frantically, pressing her lips together to hold in her reaction. Kate's solitary word confirmed Violet's thoughts.

"What?" Lila demanded.

"I don't like Leopold," Violet said, staring at the man. She spoke too loudly, and he turned her way.

Father's jaw dropped. "Violet!"

"I beg your pardon," Leopold told Vi. "I am the victim here."

"No, you aren't," Violet said. "You are the benefiter. If you actually loved your brother, I'll eat my shoe."

"Violet!" the earl snapped.

"With your brother and your evil games—do you really think you'll get off scot free? You think that Victor, Jack, Devonsly, and I—do you think we won't warn our friends off of you?"

Leopold tried laughing, but Violet was furious and she wouldn't be stopped. "How many points do you get for driving a girl to murder?"

"Violet," her father said. "Stop."

"No!" Violet turned to her father. "Celia Rosens was an innocent, stupid girl who believed in love. They played with her emotions. Leopold made Celia fall in love with him, and he dropped her."

"He did what now?" Devonsly demanded. "That sweet little thing. Why would you drop her?"

Violet answered for Leopold. "So his brother could have a chance. Leopold dropped Celia, crushing her heart, and in stepped Melrose. He stole her heart away until one of their former victims warned Celia off."

Leopold stuttered. "You can't prove it."

"No one proved anything about me and murder investigations and yet I was a suspect when your brother was found. You should have been the suspect. You're the sole heir now. You said it yo—"

Violet paused, her gaze meeting Jack's, who slowly turned to face Leopold. "You are benefiting, really." Jack clapped Leopold on the back. "Wasn't there something about a great aunt?"

Violet nodded.

"You're an only child now, aren't you? Whatever your parents have will come your way as well. No portions peeled off for little brother."

Leopold glanced between Violet and Jack. "I suppose."

"Devonsly—" Violet played with the ring on her finger, turning to the young lord. "Did you ever see Melrose with a cocktail?"

Devonsly shook his head. "Everyone knows he only drinks wine. Melrose is a weepy drunk. If he gets zozzled, it's tears and confessions, ever since we were in school. Do you remember that time when we were boys, Leo? Melrose confessed to cheating on an exam when that little beanpole came back to school with a bottle of his father's bourbon."

Leopold shot Devonsly a look. "What does my brother have to do with not drinking?"

"Celia swears she's innocent," Violet told Devonsly. "I'm not sure I've ever heard a more compelling reason to murder someone than what these brothers were doing to her."

"Violet," her father said, "this conversation is morbid. The man just lost his brother."

"But Father," Violet said to him. "It doesn't add up. It never did. Why poison someone *and* stab them? That poison was intended for you, Leopold. You can't poison a teetotaler with arsenic in gin."

Leopold shuddered, swallowing dramatically. "I suppose she intended to kill me too. Only she was discovered first."

Violet saw Jack shake his head slightly. "No," Violet said merrily, hiding her growing fury. "It still doesn't add up. Celia wouldn't have known of your late night drink habit. Not before she got here. Her father wouldn't leave her home. She's not a girl who gets to travel from house party to house party. She couldn't have known that you had that late night cocktail. Or two? Several I would guess."

"I—what—" He shook his head and then tried for a charming smile.

Violet laughed mockingly. "Your own brother was going to kill you. What, for the money? Because he loved Celia and wanted her back? You were trying to romance her again, weren't you? Making her promises in the garden. The morning after your brother was dead, you were after her."

"I thought—love—you know—"

"You don't love her." Violet laughed. "We're not that dense or that drunk, boyo. If you loved her, you'd be far more upset. Before Celia was taken in, you were romancing her. She has an aunt, doesn't she? You knew that my money was gone, but Celia's money with your solo inheritance would probably be a tidy sum."

The earl rose, standing over Vi, looming really, and he asked, "What are you doing, Violet?"

"Sir," Jack said to Father, "Violet and I both have felt like the murder didn't make sense. Who poisons and stabs? Those are murders for very different temperaments."

"So perhaps it's as you said, Melrose was attempting to murder his brother, and Celia—"

"If Celia were the killer," Violet said with a shake of her head, "then they both would have been poisoned. She had a key to your rooms in London. She'd have poisoned something and left you to your fate. It makes far more sense than to come here. But Melrose—he would need to murder you somewhere *other* than your rooms. And given the games you play with the young ladies, I am guessing you don't get all that many house party invitations."

Leopold stepped back. "Why are you saying these things?"

"Because," Jack told him, "if Celia isn't the poisoner, and it doesn't make sense that she is, then Melrose attempted to murder you. And you, sir, are the murderer of your brother. The only possible way that Celia Rosens could overpower Melrose was if he had already been poisoned and too weak to fight her. Since he didn't drink gin, and we've all agreed he didn't, Melrose intended to poison you. Rather than letting your brother kill you, you killed him first."

"You can't prove that," Leopold said coldly. "I don't have to take these accusations." He hurried towards the door to the parlor as the gong rang.

"Enjoy your self-righteous flight," Violet called. "Inspector Wright will be coming for you soon."

"He has proof that Celia Rosens killed Melrose," Leopold said, turning.

"Easily debunked now that he knows what to look for. You're trusting, of course, that Melrose was clever in his purchase," Jack told him. "How clever could he have been if you realized he had arsenic? They'll find the chemist, realize it was Melrose who purchased the poison, and the case against Celia will fall apart."

Leopold was gaping, staring at them in utter horror. With that dawning terror in his gaze, Violet asked Jack, "What if he admits to the crime and says it was self-defense?"

Stabbing with an ice pick over a poisoned bottle? Hardly self-defense, but Leopold fell for the trap in his panic. "Yes! Self-defense! It was self-defense."

Violet rolled her eyes, shook her head and sipped her cocktail as Jack told her father, "Call for Wright. Tell him what we discovered. He can come for Nelson, and Celia can go home to her family. I believe we will be witness enough to free her."

Father glanced between Jack and Violet. "I see now. I knew you were a good man, but— Vi, you chose well."

Jack took Leopold from the room while Father sent for the constables. "I need another cocktail," Violet told Victor. "This time with champagne. Reasons for celebrating abound."

Victor's head snapped around, Violet winked, and he shook his head before he sent for champagne bottles and fresh ice.

# CHAPTER NINETEEN

"You will, of course, name her after me," Violet told Kate and Victor at their wedding three days later. "Vi Junior has a delightful ring to it."

"Hush," Victor said. "We're pretending we didn't need to rush to the altar."

Violet kissed her brother's cheek and her new sister's cheek, and then lifted her champagne in salute. "Pretending though we might be, Vi Junior is *just* the name. You could also call her Pearl of Great Price. After me, of course."

"Of course." Kate had lost the sickly look. Violet was guessing that the stress of not knowing what they should do about the impending arrival had faded when Father stepped in and arranged everything for the wedding. Her eyes were bright, her dress was white and long, and the joy that radiated from her was outshone only by the joy radiating from Victor.

"You know what this means, don't you?" Violet asked Victor.

He cocked his head, waiting for an answer.

"Father realized what was happening *even* before I did. It means he was probably also aware that we framed Geoffrey with the pranks far better than Leopold framed poor Celia for the murder."

"In retrospect," Victor announced, "we shouldn't have used our own classic pranks." He wrapped his arm around Kate's waist. "I wonder what I would do in such a situation."

"Our children will be delightful, like me," Kate told Victor, who choked on his laughter.

"Darling," Violet told her new sister, "you have sullied your family tree with Victor. Returning to young Geoffrey, this does mean Father punished Geoffrey knowing he was innocent."

Victor shrugged, entirely unrepentant.

"It also means that Father is probably far more aware of what we do than we knew. How long do you think he knew we were V. V. Twinnings?"

Victor took a deep breath in and considered. "Possibly within days of our not asking Father for more money. We were doing that quite frequently before our books."

That was Vi's guess as well. She saw they were agreed, and they both turned to look at their father, who was laughing with Isolde, Tomas, and Gerald.

"It also means," Victor said, "he let Aunt Agatha have us. How long did it take until after he married Lady Eleanor that we were spending more time with dear Aggie than at home?"

"Not long," she mused. "He's always known what Lady Eleanor was."

Victor kissed Kate on her temple. "Violet, I am going to make a rash statement."

She rubbed her hands together, awaiting the revelation.

"It is possible that Father is almost as witty as you. I like to think I get my laziness from him. If he were a touch less idle, we might have had to be good children instead of the devils we were. We might have also been raised by him and Lady Eleanor rather than Aunt Agatha."

"Are," Kate inserted. "You *are* devils. You're adults and you framed a child to watch him squirm."

"Touché," Victor said to his bride.

"It's good for him," Violet added. Her attention was caught, and she gasped. "Now I hate to kiss and run, but your mother is terrifying, Kate dear. She is also aimed this way, so I'm off for cake and canapés. Congratulations again, darling, on acquiring such a wonderful sister."

Violet was chased away by the sound of their laughter. There was a lot of laughter this fine autumn morning. It seemed as though the sun wanted to shine down on the couple and their loved ones. Violet wrapped her arm through Jack's, grinning at her complete joy in the day's events, and Jack made it all better simply by putting his hand over hers.

He smiled down at her. "Are you happy?"

Violet nodded, grinning up at him. "Of course. It is just like Victor to draw attention from my birthday with his shenanigans."

"I didn't forget," Jack said, kissing her brow. "Are you prepared to be an aunt?"

"I think I shall have to be a sister first," Violet told him, her gaze fixing on Geoffrey. "Before we spoil Violet Junior, shall we de-spoil young Geoffrey?"

Jack followed Violet's gaze to where Geoffrey was watching the wedding party from the sidelines, a sour expression on his face. He had a glass of champagne, but he wasn't enjoying it. He seemed to be entirely displeased by the happy event.

Their gazes moved from Geoffrey to Lord Devonsly whispering sweet nothings into a blushing Celia Rosens's ear and on to Lady Eleanor pretending joy as Victor forever removed his inheritance from Geoffrey's grasp.

From them, Violet turned to Lila and Denny. He was leaning towards his wife, smiling at her in that lazy way, and then he lifted her hand to his mouth, turned it over, and placed a kiss on the inside of her wrist.

"He loves her so," Violet said, watching her friend say something to Denny that had him laughing.

"He does," Jack said. She turned to him and found it was only her who had been watching Lila and Denny. Jack, on the other hand, was entirely fixated on Violet, and there was little doubt that the protestation of love was for anyone else.

"She loves him as well," Violet said and found each of her fingertips kissed.

## The End

Hullo, my friends, I have so much gratitude for you reading my books and enjoying them. Are there words enough to explain how that feels? Almost as wonderful are reviews, and indie folks, like myself, need them desperately! If you wouldn't mind, I would be so grateful for a review.

The sequel to this book, *Obsidian Murder* is currently available.

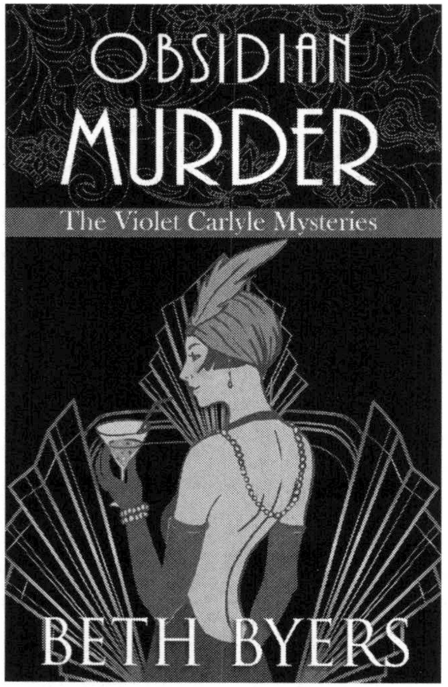


**Bonfire Night 1924.**

Violet, Victor, and friends intend to celebrate an evening with cocktails, bonfires, and fireworks. What they don't intend is to find a body instead of their Guy Fawkes. What's even more baffling? The obsidian blade. Once again, the friends delve into a wicked crime. Tensions rise as they realize that murder wasn't the only game afoot during the celebration.

Order Here.

I am delighted to announce the arrival of my new historical mystery series, The Poison Ink Mysteries.

**July 1936.**

When Georgette Dorothy Marsh's dividends fall along with the banks, she decides to write a book. Her only hope is to bring her account out of overdraft and possibly buy some hens. The problem is that she has so little imagination she uses her neighbors for inspiration.

She little expects anyone to realize what she's done. So when *Chronicles of Harper's Bend* becomes a bestseller, her neighbors are questing to find out just who this "Joe Johns" is and punish him.

Things escalate beyond what anyone would imagine when one of her prominent characters turns up dead. It seems that the fictional end

Georgette had written for the character spurred a real-life murder. Now to find the killer before it is discovered who the author is and she becomes the next victim.

If you'd like to a copy, click here. Or keep on flipping for a preview.

FYI, I write under my real name, Amanda A. Allen, as well. If you like books with a paranormal twist, you'll find I've written plenty! Books and updates for both names are available through my newsletter. If you'd like to sign up, click here.

If you want book updates, you could follow me on Facebook by clicking here for Beth Byers. Or here for Amanda A. Allen.

# ALSO BY BETH BYERS

**The Violet Carlyle Cozy Historical Mysteries**

Murder & the Heir

Murder at Kennington House

Murder at the Folly

A Merry Little Murder

New Year's Madness: A Short Story Anthology

Valentine's Madness: A Short Story Anthology

Murder Among the Roses

Murder in the Shallows

Gin & Murder

Murder at the Ladies Club

Weddings Vows & Murder

**The Poison Ink Mysteries**

A Historical Cozy Mystery

Death by the Book

Death Witnessed

Death by Blackmail

Death Misconstrued

Deathly Ever After

**The 2nd Chance Diner Mysteries**

Spaghetti, Meatballs, & Murder

Cookies & Catastrophe

(found in the Christmas boxset, The Three Carols of Cozy Christmas Murder)

Poison & Pie

Double Mocha Murder

Cinnamon Rolls & Cyanide

Tea & Temptation

Donuts & Danger

Scones & Scandal

Lemonade & Loathing

Wedding Cake & Woe

Honeymoons & Honeydew

The Pumpkin Problem

**The Brightwater Bay Mysteries**

*(co-written with Carolyn L. Dean and Angela Blackmoore)*

A Little Taste of Murder

(found in the Christmas boxset, The Three Carols of Cozy Christmas Murder)

A Tiny Dash of Death

A Sweet Spoonful of Cyanide

# ALSO BY AMANDA A. ALLEN

**Mystic Cove Mommy Mysteries**

Bedtimes & Broomsticks

Runes & Roller Skates

Banshees and Babysitters

Hobgoblins and Homework

Christmas and Curses

Valentines & Valkyries

**The Rue Hallow Mysteries**

Hallow Graves

Hungry Graves

Lonely Graves

Sisters and Graves

Yule Graves

Fated Graves

Ruby Graves

**The Inept Witches Mysteries**

*(co-written with Auburn Seal)*

Inconvenient Murder

Moonlight Murder

Bewitched Murder

Presidium Vignettes (with Rue Hallow)

Prague Murder

Paris Murder

Murder By Degrees

# PREVIEW OF DEATH BY THE BOOK

## Chapter One

### GEORGETTE MARSH

Georgette Dorothy Marsh stared at the statement from her bank with a dawning horror. The dividends had been falling, but this...this wasn't livable. She bit down on the inside of her lip and swallowed frantically. *What was she going to do?* Tears were burning in the back of her eyes, and her heart was racing frantically.

There wasn't enough for—for—anything. Not for cream for her tea or resoling her shoes or firewood for the winter. Georgette glanced out the window, remembered it was spring, and realized that something must be done.

Something, but *what*?

"Miss?" Eunice said from the doorway, "the tea at Mrs. Wilkes is this afternoon. You asked me to remind you."

Georgette nodded, frantically trying to hide her tears from her maid, but the servant had known Georgette since the day of her birth, caring for her from her infancy to the current day.

"What has happened?"

"The...the dividends," Georgette breathed. She didn't have enough air to speak clearly. "The dividends. It's not enough."

Eunice's head cocked as she examined her mistress and then she said, "Something must be done."

"But what?" Georgette asked, biting down on her lip again. *Hard.*

* * * * *

## CHARLES AARON

"Uncle?"

Charles Aaron glanced up from the stack of papers on his desk at his nephew some weeks after Georgette Marsh had written her book in a fury of desperation. It was Robert Aaron who had discovered the book, and it was Charles Aaron who would give it life.

Robert had been working at Aaron & Luther Publishing House for a year before Georgette's book appeared in the mail, and he read the slush pile of books that were submitted by new authors before either of the partners stepped in. It was an excellent rewarding work when you found that one book that separated itself from the pile, and Robert got that thrill of excitement every time he found a book that had a touch of *something*. It was the very feeling that had Charles himself pursuing a career in publishing and eventually creating his own firm.

It didn't seem to matter that Charles had his long history of discovering authors and their books. Familiarity had most definitely *not* led to contempt. He was, he had to admit, in love with reading—fiction especially—and the creative mind. He had learned that some of the books he found would speak only to him.

Often, however, some he loved would become best sellers. With the best sellers, Charles felt he was sharing a delightful secret with the world. There was magic in discovering a new writer. A contagious sort of magic that had infected Robert. There was nothing that Charles enjoyed more than hearing someone recommend a book he'd published to another.

"You've found something?"

Robert shrugged, but he also handed the manuscript over a smile right on the edge of his lips and shining eyes that flicked to the manuscript over and over again. "Yes, I think so." He wasn't confident enough yet to feel certain, but Charles had noticed for some time that Robert was getting closer and closer to no longer needing anyone to guide him.

"I'll look it over soon."

It was the end of the day and Charles had a headache building behind his eyes. He always did on the days when he had to deal with the bestseller Thomas Spencer. He was too successful for his own good and expected any publishing company to bend entirely to his will.

Robert watched Charles load the manuscript into his satchel, bouncing just a little before he pulled back and cleared his throat. The boy—man, Charles supposed—smoothed his suit, flashed a grin, and left the office. Leaving for the day wasn't a bad plan. He took his satchel and—as usual—had dinner at his club before retiring to a corner of the room with an overstuffed armchair, an Old-Fashioned, and his pipe.

Charles glanced around the club, noting the other regulars. Most of them were bachelors who found it easier to eat at the club than to employ a cook. Every once in a while there was a family man who'd escaped the house for an evening with the gents, but for the most part —it was bachelors like himself.

When Charles opened the neat pages of 'Joseph Jones's *The Chronicles of Harper's Bend,* he intended to read only a small portion of the book. To get a feel for what Robert had seen and perhaps determine whether it was worth a more thorough look. After a few pages, Charles decided upon just a few more. A few more pages after that, and he left his club to return home and finish the book by his own fire.

It might have been early summer, but they were also in the middle of a ferocious storm. Charles preferred the crackle of fire wherever possible when he read, as well as a good cup of tea. There was no question that the book was well done. There was no question that Charles would be contacting the author and making an offer on the book. *The Chronicles of Harper's Bend* was, in fact, so captivating in its honesty, he couldn't quite decide whether this author loved the small towns of England or despised them. He rather felt it might be both.

Either way, it was quietly sarcastic and so true to the little village that raised Charles Aaron that he felt he might turn the page and discover the old woman who'd lived next door to his parents or the vicar of the church he'd attended as a boy. Charles felt as though he knew the people stepping off the pages.

Yes, Charles thought, yes. This one, he thought, *this* would be a best seller. Charles could feel it in his bones. He tapped out his pipe into the ashtray. This would be one of those books he looked back on with pride at having been the first to know that this book was the next big thing. Despite the lateness of the hour, Charles approached his bedroom with an energized delight. A letter would be going out in the morning.

~

* * * * *

## GEORGETTE MARSH

It was on the very night that Charles read the *Chronicles* that Miss Georgette Dorothy Marsh paced, once again, in front of her fireplace. The wind whipped through the town of Bard's Crook sending a flurry of leaves swirling around the graves in the small churchyard and then shooing them down to a small lane off of High Street where the elderly Mrs. Henry Parker had been awake for some time. She had woken worried over her granddaughter who was recovering too slowly from the measles.

The wind rushed through the cottages at the end of the lane, causing the gate at the Wilkes house to rattle. Dr. Wilkes and his wife were curled up together in their bed sharing warmth in the face of the changing weather. A couple much in love, snuggling into their beds on a windy evening was a joy for them both.

The leaves settled into a pile in the corner of the picket fence right at the very last cottage on that lane of Miss Georgette Dorothy Marsh. Throughout most of Bard's Crook, people were sleeping. Their hot water bottles were at the ends of their beds, their blankets were piled high, and they went to bed prepared for another day. The unseasonable chill had more than one household enjoying a warm cup of milk at bedtime, though not Miss Marsh's economizing household.

Miss Marsh, unlike the others, was not asleep. She didn't have a fire as she was quite at the end of her income and every adjustment must be made. If she were going to be honest with herself, and she very much didn't want to be—she was past the end of her income. Her account had become overdraft, her dividends had dried up, and it might be time to recognize that her last-ditch effort of writing a book about her neighbors had not been successful.

She had looked at the lives of folks like Anthony Trollope who both worked and wrote novels and Louisa May Alcott who wrote to relieve the stress of her life and to help bring in financial help. As much as Georgette loved to read, and she did, she loved the idea that somewhere out there an author was using their art to restart their lives. There was a romance to being a writer, but she wondered just how many writers were pragmatic behind the fairytales they crafted. It wasn't, Georgette thought, going to be her story like Louisa May Alcott. Georgette was going to do something else.

"Miss Georgie," Eunice said, "I can hear you. You'll catch something dreadful if you don't sleep." The sound of muttering chased Georgie, who had little doubt Eunice was complaining about catching something dreadful herself.

"I'm sorry, Eunice," Georgie called. "I—" Georgie opened the door to her bedroom and faced the woman. She had worked for Mr. and Mrs. Marsh when Georgie had been born and in all the years of loss and change, Eunice had never left Georgie. Even now when the economies made them both uncomfortable. "Perhaps—"

"It'll be all right in the end, Miss Georgie. Now to bed with you."

Georgette did not, however, go to bed. Instead, she pulled out her pen and paper and listed all of the things she might do to further economize. They had a kitchen garden already, and it provided the vast majority of what they ate. They did their own mending and did not buy new clothes. They had one goat that they milked and made their own cheese. Though Georgette had to recognize that she rather feared goats. They were, of all creatures, devils. They would just randomly knock one over.

Georgie shivered and refused to consider further goats. Perhaps she could tutor someone? She thought about those she knew and realized that no one in Bard's Crook would hire the quiet Georgette Dorothy Marsh to influence their children. The village's wallflower and cipher? Hardly a legitimate option for any caring parent. Georgette was all too aware of what her neighbors thought of her. She rose again, pacing more quietly as she considered and rejected her options.

Georgie paced until quite late and then sat down with her pen and paper and wondered if she should try again with her writing. Something else. Something with more imagination. She had started her book with fits until she'd landed on practicing writing by describing an episode of her village. It had grown into something more, something beyond Bard's Crook with just conclusions to the lives she saw around her.

When she'd started *The Chronicles of Harper's Bend,* she had been more desperate than desirous of a career in writing. Once again, she recognized that she must do something and she wasn't well-suited to anything but writing. There were no typist jobs in Bard's Crook, no secretarial work. The time when rich men paid for companions for their wives or elderly mothers was over, and the whole of the world was struggling to survive, Georgette included.

She'd thought of going to London for work, but if she left her snug little cottage, she'd have to pay for lodging elsewhere. Georgie sighed into her palm and then went to bed. There was little else to do at that moment. Something, however, must be done.

**This book is currently available.**

❀ Created with Vellum

Made in the USA
San Bernardino, CA
16 September 2019